This Large Print Book carries the Seal of Approval of N.A.V.H.

Barefoot Brides

Center Point
Large Print

Sequel to **THE BAREFOOT BELIEVERS**

ANNIE JONES

Barefoot Brides

CENTER POINT PUBLISHING
THORNDIKE, MAINE

This Center Point Large Print edition
is published in the year 2009 by
arrangement with Harlequin Books, S.A.

The text of this Large Print edition is unabridged.
In other aspects, this book may vary
from the original edition.
Printed in the United States of America.
Set in 16-point Times New Roman type.

ISBN: 978-1-60285-355-3

Library of Congress Cataloging-in-Publication Data

Jones, Annie, 1957–
    Barefoot brides / Annie Jones. — Large print ed.
        p. cm. — (Barefoot series ; bk. 2)
    Originally published: Don Mills, Ont.: Steeple Hill, 2009.
    "Center Point large print edition" — Verso t.p.
    ISBN 978-1-60285-355-3 (library binding : alk. paper)
    1. Large type books. I. Title. II. Series.

PS3560.O45744B38 2009
813′.54—dc22
2008044146

For Carrie and Chris,
With love and prayers for your own
happily ever after!

Abducted Child Found Living in Same Town as Birth Family
R. Hunt Diamante
Sun Times editor

Santa Sofia, Florida. Dorothy "Dodie" Cromwell never gave up hope of finding the daughter her ex-husband abducted from the family home near Atlanta, Georgia, more than thirty years ago. Little did she know that, for much of that time, she and her two older daughters, Dr. Kate Cromwell and Jo Cromwell, both formerly of Atlanta, had spent their summer vacations in Santa Sofia just a few miles from where the missing child was being raised by local fishing boat icon and fry cook, William Jay Weatherby, more commonly known as "Billy J" of Billy J's Bait Shack and Seafood Buffet.

"She worked as a caretaker of the Cromwell's summer cottage and the one across the street from it since she was sixteen. She never met them face-to-face until they came down looking to sell the place two months ago," reported Weatherby of his foster daughter, Maxine, who works in property management. He had taken the child in when her biological father abandoned her in Santa Sofia when she was still a toddler.

The four women realized their connection when they matched a photograph found in the Cromwell cottage to one already in Weatherby's possession.

"Proof was right there on the wall of the Bait Shack, right next to the place where we put up the dinner specials." Weatherby referred to a framed photo, which he had been told was of his daughter and a distant relative who no longer had any wish to see the child but in fact was of Mrs. Cromwell and her baby taken the day before the abduction. "I feel the Lord's hand in this, I tell you what."

Chapter One

"That's it?" Kate Cromwell used her antique walking stick, which she had relied upon as a cane since having her foot broken a month earlier, to wedge her way between her sisters. "Surely that's not the whole piece? The story of our lives reduced to a few poorly researched, mistake-ridden paragraphs? I mean, really, most of us weren't even interviewed by that . . . that . . ."

"Journalist." Moxie Weatherby, whose legal name was not now nor had it ever been Maxine, spoke the word the way she might have said *cockroach.* Then she appeared to reconsider. Cockroaches weren't all that bad, after all, to a person raised in Florida. "Or should I say so-called journalist?"

"Yes, thank you, Moxie." Kate leaned over the kitchen table where her mother and Billy J had spread the pages of the local paper out for all to see. "This *so-called* journalist reduced our whole story down to 'I feel the Lord's hand in this, I tell you what'?"

"There are worse things that could be said about people's lives, Kate." Despite her wise but decidedly snooty-sounding comment, Jo stretched up on her tanned toes and strained to get a better look. "Though I daresay the man could have found so much more to flesh out the story if he'd just made a little effort."

"By interviewing *you*, no doubt?" Kate meant it as a tease. Only after seeing the fleeting but very real flash of unhappiness in her younger, blonder and more conventionally pretty sister's face did she realize she'd hit a nerve.

She winced. As a doctor and more recently a patient, she should have had more compassion. As a sister? She wasn't quite so cautious about Jo's "nobody ever pays enough attention to me" complex.

"At least you got your title worked into the mix. I'm just one of two sisters 'formerly of Atlanta.' " Jo pouted in her perfect not-too-pouty way. Everything Jo did, from being one of the most successful up-and-coming Realtors in Atlanta to chucking it all to work for the Lord at Traveler's Wayside Chapel, was done to perfection.

What did Jo have to be put out about? Kate was the one with the rekindled romance—that still hadn't quite seemed to spark into full blaze —with hometown handyman, Vince Merchant. Not to mention her new start as a partner in the local Urgent Care Clinic. And the fact that she was doing all this with a foot basically smashed to smithereens thanks to their own mother's careless driving?

Of the pair of them Kate did think her own story was the more interesting, giving *her* the right to feel more insulted by the lack of recognition. She demonstrated that fact by angling her shoulder in to block her sister's view.

Jo gave Kate a shove, in that "loving" way the sisters had with one another.

Kate almost fell *splat* on her backside.

Jo pretended not to notice.

Kate clomped backward until she got her balance, thumping her cane on the old linoleum floor of the circa 1940s cottage.

"Careful. We don't want a repeat of what happened on the front porch!" Dodie scolded Kate, who wanted to blurt out "it's not my fault" but knew they'd take her to mean the big gaping hole in the front porch was not her fault—when clearly, it *was*.

If Kate had heeded the signs Moxie had put on the front porch warning them not to use it, Kate would never have fallen through the rotting wood. But if she hadn't fallen through, she would never have drawn the attention of Vince Merchant, who came charging across the street to her rescue.

Vince Merchant.

Kate sighed.

Everyone looked at her.

11

Kate's cheeks felt as if someone had just opened the valve on a steam radiator right underneath her. She cleared her throat and banged her cane on the floor again.

"Don't you rattle your saber at me, big sister. The ankle I sprained getting into the cottage on the first day here is completely healed so I can outrun you now." This time Jo used her slightly more curvy hips to push her way in past her older, more slender sister.

"Use your brains, girl," Kate shot back, recovering her usual feistiness. "Don't think I'd let a little deal like multiple fractures, metal pins and detached tendons still awaiting further surgery keep me from relishing my place in the Cromwell family pecking order."

"As what?" Moxie scoffed. "Chief gherkin?"

"Huh?" She'd spent her lifetime running away from her guilt over her youngest sister's abduction and now that they had found each other she had a hard time reconciling that child to this now-confident young woman. "Did you just call me a—"

"*Pecking* order, Moxie," Jo enunciated each syllable so that her version sounded very little like Kate's quickly blurted out pi-kn o'ger. "Not pickle jar!"

"I can't help it if y'all talk funny," Moxie argued in an accent decidedly less Southern than Jo's or Kate's or Dodie's thick Georgia—

which everyone agreed sounded a bit like Jaw-jaw to the untrained ear—drawl. "I heard her tell you to use your *brines* and that she wouldn't let a little *dill* stop her, then she carried on about relish and my mind just naturally went that way."

"Definitely not kosher, baby sister." Jo's green eyes sparkled at the overblown corn pone imitation of their accents.

"How was I to know my own sister would go sour on me so fast?" Moxie lamented with a laugh.

Jo stepped back, relinquishing her spot to Kate at last. "Oh, I have news for you, as far as this family is concerned—"

"As far as this family is concerned—" Dodie rustled the paper still open in her hands "—it's a sisterhood, girls, not a competition."

"Yes, ma'am." The three sisters exchanged a look so sugary it could have candied a hot garlic dill—and left just as odd an aftertaste for Kate.

She *loved* her sisters.

What's more, she wanted to *like* them . . .

Moxie wiggled into the space left by Jo's retreat.

But they sure did make it hard for her!

"Does it say continued on page so-and-so at the bottom?" Moxie wanted to know.

Dodie looked up and down the length of the page, shaking her head. She glanced at the page

13

facing the story. She thumbed through the sparse offering of sections. Then, having not found anything more about her family, she hoisted the paper up and searched the table underneath. Perhaps she thought some of the greasy inked words might have slid from the pages and now lay strewn across the plastic tablecloth. "That's the whole article."

"Can't be. Talked to that man for thirty minutes on the phone," Billy J muttered. "Not so's you'd know it to read that mess. Turned the Bait Shack Seafood Buffet into the Bait Shack *and* Seafood Buffet. As if we was selling chum and nightcrawlers and right alongside crawfish and calamari!"

"You mean you're not?" Dodie looked at him with a mix of awe and innocence.

Jo caught Kate's eye, and they both had to stifle a giggle. Even after all the things they had gone through and despite all their differences, it was good to know they still shared the same snarky sense of humor.

"What?" Billy J scowled at the gray-haired woman at his side.

Kate opened her mouth to rally to her mother's defense, which wasn't hard to do considering the way Billy J batter-dipped and deep-fried everything but the flatware down at the Bait Shack—making it hard to distinguish exactly what was on your plate at any given time.

"I'll have you know, woman—" Billy J spoke first, but whatever it was he wanted Dodie to know got lost in a red-faced bout of smoker's cough that carried the same intense blustering mood as his words but sounded more like the barking of an asthmatic seal.

"I think you have grounds to call for a retraction, Daddy." Moxie patted her father's back, pounded it, really, as though that would actually quell his coughing fit as she said, "I'll see to that."

"What about the rest of it?" The coughing did begin to subside. "Fry cook! The man called me a fry cook!"

"I know, Daddy." The younger sister's tender but firm ministrations continued. She'd done this before. A lot. It showed in her resolute technique, in her calm persistence and in the anxious concern in her eyes.

"I'm a restaurateur!"

"I *know,* Daddy." More pounding. Less coughing.

"And a renowned fisherman, not a fishing boat icon. Makes me sound like a cartoon painted on the sides of boats up and down the Emerald Coast!"

Kate had to hold her tongue to keep from saying she could actually imagine the big-bellied fellow, with his white beard and captain's hat complete with parrot feather in the band, that way. She wasn't unsympathetic. She understood the man had both self-esteem and health situations, but she didn't have much patience with him today.

He'd done this all to himself. He had been the one to take up so much of the editor's time that no one else had been given a chance. Plus, even though his physician and his daughter had asked him repeatedly, he would not give up his cigarettes. The man behaved a bit like a cartoon character, like an icon that would live forever, and she was tempted to tell him just that. If he would ever give anyone a chance to break in between coughs and comments.

"I have half a mind to complain to the editor and make him redo the whole article," Billy J blustered.

Moxie pointed to the byline. "It says he *is* the new editor, Daddy."

Billy J yanked the front page out of the jumble of pages and frowned at the masthead. "Reinhardt Media Enterprises?"

"It's a big media conglomerate." Jo jumped in to explain. "Very powerful. Very influential. Very—"

"Bad news," Moxie concluded. "Bad news for our little paper and bad news for our little town."

No one seemed to have an argument for that. How could they, staring at this awful piece of supposed journalism about their remarkable reunion? Not to mention the amateurish mess of a photo they had run with it.

"Forget the article and the editor. *I* want a retraction of this picture." Jo flicked her polished nail against the edge of the page, right beside the spot where the left side of her face had been cut out of the grainy black-and-white shot. The vivacious, blond thirty-five-year-old, so meticulous about her hair, her outfits, her shoes—especially her shoes—had been reduced to a blur. Or more precisely, half a blur.

"It was the only photo I had of all of us together," Dodie offered sheepishly. "Guess it didn't translate well into newsprint. To be fair, it's not the most accurate likeness of any of us."

That was easy for her mother to accept, Kate had to think, because *her* inaccuracy made her teased-up gray hair helmet look soft and wind-tossed, like an old-time movie starlet's. Took almost a decade off the woman's sixty-six years. Besides, with all of them pressed in adoringly around her, Dodie came off slightly less plump and infinitely more substantial than the flustered and flighty Southern Mee-Maw—even though she didn't have a single grandchild to call her Mee-Maw or Nana or Grammy-Dodie or whatever cutesy name its little heart desired—everyone instantly took her for.

"Now, pretty Miss Jo has a point here, y'all.

17

As photos go, it don't do none of us justice." Billy J's chair groaned beneath his weight as he scooted in to get a closer look. "No one can tell me that I really look like *that*. Do I?"

Everyone in the room made some kind of noise, but none of them sounded anything at all like an actual answer one way or another.

If the old fellow had been the sensitive type, he'd have been hurt, certainly. But then if he'd been even a tad more sensitive, he'd have gathered the truth about his appearance from all the children through the years who had mistaken him for Santa Claus on vacation.

He shook his head and scratched behind his ear, making the white-and-black captain's hat, which he wore so much people didn't know if he was hiding baldness or just had the world's worst case of hat-hair underneath it, bob up and down. That sent the parrot's feather in the brim bouncing.

"You look like you always do, Daddy. Just the way you are supposed to look," Moxie reassured him with a pat on his back. "I just hope people aren't sitting in kitchens and diners all over Santa Sofia this morning saying the same thing about the rest of us."

She had a point. The three sisters, and you had to squint to make sure there were three of them gathered behind the two older folks at the center of the photo, did not fare well.

There was Jo, a power-selling business dynamo who had just come to the realization that money and success and, yes, even great shoes, were no substitute for service and feeling that what you did in life mattered. She'd suffered the worst in the reproduction of the family portrait as the light on her short blond hair made it blend into her face and with the paleness of her suit jacket left her not just unrecognizable but barely discernible.

A lack of distinction that the middle sister, the one left behind by their father and left to her own devices by her mother, would feel to her very core.

And Kate. She had become a doctor after years of searching for her true calling, including leaving behind her one true love, none other than her porch rescuer Vince Merchant. She usually radiated good health, athleticism and a take-charge attitude. But anyone reading the *Sun Times* today would describe her as birdlike and practically ancient.

In the photo, the sun streaks in her brown hair could easily have passed for premature gray. The fact that she had one hand on a cane because of the accidental foot injury—which was a nice way of saying her mother had tried to run away from home and ran over Kate's foot instead—that had brought her to Santa Sofia to recover in the first place did not help.

Then there was Moxie.

Poor baby.

Kate felt a rush of genuine empathy for the youngest sister.

Squished between Jo and Kate, both vying for prominence next to their mom, Moxie had to squat to get her round chin between the heads of Billy J and Dodie. Not only did that require she suffer the discomfort of the hair helmet and ever-present hat but she had to twist her face just so to avoid the indignity of having a feather go up her nose. To top it off, nothing of her thick ponytail, in a mix of colors she liked to call *beach-blah-nd,* showed. That left only her bangs in view, suggesting she'd cut her hair by putting a cereal bowl on her head and merrily whacking away at anything that stuck out.

Moxie looked as if she wanted to be anywhere but there.

"Let me see that article again. Did that hack even mention my great food at fair prices?" Billy J coughed again, lightly this time, as he created a commotion fighting with the pages. "I went over that and made him recite it back to me word for word. He assured me that he would put the Bait Shack in the piece."

"And he did." Kate ran her index finger line by line over the scant few rows of smudgy black ink as if she had to double-check that she had missed something in the bland four-paragraph summation. "He didn't even mention that I've joined the Urgent Care Clinic and will be setting up a part-time private practice after the first of the year."

"If you last that long," Jo muttered into her raised coffee mug.

"What's that supposed to mean?" Kate narrowed her eyes, one hand still on the paper, the other on her ever-present cane.

"Oh, nothing," Jo said soft and *almost* sweet. "Except maybe the man didn't mention it in his article because he's heard of your reputation for running away when things get too intense, Scat-Kat Katie."

"Don't call me that." Kate did not protest that she had changed, or at least was trying to, but the muted anguish in her words got the message across.

"Don't even bring up names!" Moxie put her hand to her forehead then impulsively swept it back to loosen her almost-always-present ponytail to let her hair down. She fluffed and smoothed the heavy strands even as she promised, "If I ever meet this R. Hunt Diamante in person, I am going to give him a piece of my mind!"

Everyone looked at her in a medley of disbelief, amusement and maybe just a dash of hope that she would muster the backbone to do just what she said.

Moxie might be mouthy but she was also generous to a fault and more likely to give of herself than to give anyone a strong talking-to.

"Or . . ." she said, twisting her fingers in the hem of her "I'm hooked on Billy J's Bait Shack" T-shirt, "at least I'll hand him my business card so he can get my name and occupation right."

"Call me when you do that." Jo put a sympathetic hand on her sister's shoulder.

"So you can send your boyfriend, the wonderful minister man, around to lend counsel?" Dodie asked, the eagerness in her eyes clearly more for the prospect of Jo admitting that handsome Travis Brandt was officially her boyfriend than about him helping Moxie deliver what Southerners fondly call a "come to Jesus" message to R. Hunt Diamante.

"No, so I can go with her and cheer her on," Jo shot back, ignoring the blatant question about her relationship with Travis altogether.

"You're just hoping you'll get a second shot at getting your picture in the paper." Kate pointed to the white blob that should have resembled Jo.

"Well, *I* don't want my picture in the paper again, but I wouldn't mind having the facts corrected." Moxie tried to keep from sounding over-wrought, which she clearly wasn't, but sometimes she came off that way because of her age and her still-girlishly chubby face. Besides, as the daughter of a character like Billy J, a lot of folks around town probably thought she had every right to be overwrought most of the time anyway. "I have worked hard most of my life to get where I am, to be more than just Billy J's daughter, and everyone in town knows that— except, apparently, the new editor of our only newspaper!"

"That's just the problem, isn't it?" Kate sighed. "Everybody in town already *does* know you. But me?"

Jo gave her the ol' arched-eyebrow routine as if to say, "What *about* you? Not everything is about *you!*"

"I'm trying to get established here." Kate shut her eyes and exhaled impatiently. "And in partnership with *your* boyfriend, Moxie, so he'll have more free time for you. So there's something to benefit you in them mentioning the clinic and my practice—"

"I didn't ask you to do that." Now Moxie *did* sound overwrought. "I didn't ask you to join the clinic or free up Lionel's time or do me any favors, Kate, so—"

"Might as well learn it now, Moxie, you don't have to *ask* Kate for anything." Jo angled her shoulders so that it gave the impression of a united front, the younger girls against the eldest. "She's always too happy to rush in to the rescue, whether you want her to or not and—"

"Stop it! Would you two stop it?" Billy J thun-

23

dered at last, smacking his hand against his knee. Another burst of soft coughing followed then subsided. "Land's sake, you sound like—"

"They sound like—" Dodie stood slowly, almost choking on the last word "—sisters."

The room fell utterly silent, charged with a tension that felt almost electric.

Dodie wiped away a tear. "After all these years and after all that heartache, my girls sound like the sisters they were always meant to be. Please don't tell them to be quiet, Billy. To me it's the sweetest sound I've ever heard."

More silence, this time charged with some lesser energy, more like the static cling generated by two socks hot from the dryer.

Finally Moxie, for whom this sister business must still have been very new and very odd, frowned. "So let me get this straight . . . you *want* us to keep bickering?"

"She wants us to be sweet and act like sisters," Kate corrected, giving the final word on the matter.

Then Jo, never willing to let her sister *have* that last word, summed it up for all of them. "Given the reality of our lives as they are, not as they should have been, she may just have to choose one or the other. We can be sweet or we can act like sisters, but for the time being, I don't think we can do both."

Chapter Two

Shortly before noon, Jo stood at the edge of the ocean with her sandals in her hands, her feet in the sand and her heart in her throat. Just a few hundred feet away, the sounds from Traveler's Wayside Chapel mixed with the rush and swoosh of the waves lapping at the shore.

She could hear the voices, mostly male voices, laughing and talking. By now Travis Brandt had probably just finished dishing up a hot meal to the homeless and working poor or anyone who just needed a little warmth and kindness.

In a few minutes she would go to the chapel to talk to him about her plans. She so wanted to start again, to try to be the kind of person she believed God—and the people near and dear to her heart—wanted her to be.

And she would probably fall short.

Be sweet.

Her mother had admonished her to do that her whole life.

Act like sisters.

She didn't know if she could.

Jo had tried. She felt the Lord knew how hard

she had tried to be a good sister and a good daughter only to find herself feeling . . . superfluous.

No, that didn't sound right. Jo wasn't *super* anything.

Her whole life she'd been a spare part. Something left over when their father had taken the baby and their mother had fit the pieces of their life back together again.

The role of mother's little helper had been filled to overflowing by Kate the great. And while to most onlookers Jo might have seemed the logical choice for baby of the family, that spot had remained forever unfilled—a giant gaping hole in their hearts and in the very fabric of their family dynamic because of Moxie's abduction.

And now Moxie was back in her rightful place and Kate had taken strides to establish herself in the town where their mother wanted to live out the rest of her life. And Jo?

When she had decided to change her priorities and look to the Lord for her guidance, she thought she'd really go places. Yet Jo still had unfinished business in Atlanta, though no real *job* here or there. She had a new man in her life but he didn't seem to have much room for her in his. She talked a good plan but so far hadn't found anyone to listen to her.

In short, despite turning the driving force in

26

her life over to God, Jo had gotten nowhere.

That had to change. She had to step out in faith and . . . do what? If only she had a clear message, some guidance, a light to shine on the right path to take.

"But I'm hungry. I don't want a nap!"

The voice of a little boy whining startled her from her fit of anxiety. Jo turned and watched a young mother tugging a child along the beach.

"I want something to eat!"

Jo did not know if they had a home to go to for that promised nap or means of getting the meal the boy needed. What she did know was that they were heading *away* from, not *toward,* the chapel.

That troubled her.

Very few women sought out the shelter of the chapel these days, though some attended Sunday service. That dropped off considerably after tourist season when the clusters of visiting families no longer filled up the pews.

Sometimes she saw them at the free breakfasts, women with children in worn clothes and shoes with holes in the toes. Given the ebb of jobs and business away from Santa Sofia this time of year, a fair percentage of which would not come back with the few returning tourists next season, Jo knew they were out there. She knew they needed help just as much as she wanted to help them. If they would just give her—an outsider— a chance, she could make a difference in their lives.

That's why she had asked Moxie to meet her here today. Jo wanted to form an outreach to the underserved women of the community and her mother wanted her to be more sisterly. Two birds. One stone.

"I just hope she doesn't end up wanting to throw rocks at me," she whispered.

Be sweet. Be sisterly. Be the person God and your mother want you to be.

Jo shut her eyes and gave a silent prayer for help in doing it all.

A large, warm hand cupped the curve of her shoulder.

"Travis!" She whipped around, as flustered as if he had caught her ogling cutie-pie surfer dudes —not that there were any around, and even if there were, that one of them would be more ogle-worthy than the former pro-athlete turned beach-preacher himself.

He tipped his head toward the woman and child. "One of yours?"

"One of my what?" Jo squinted against the sun's bright glare.

"One of the women you had in mind when you came up with the idea of doing this . . ." He held his open hand to her, obviously encouraging her to finish the sentence, to tell him just exactly what she had in mind for a proposed women's ministry.

"A Bible study?"

"You're asking me?"

"No." She threw her hands up as though she wanted to shove the very notion out of the picture.

Then she paused and reconsidered. Of all the people on the planet whom she should ask about this effort, Travis was the one who might have real answers. Or at least be able to provide that solid guidance, that light on the right path she had prayed to receive.

"Well . . . maybe." She dropped her hands to her side and sighed, then finally gave up and recanted entirely. "Yes. Yes, I am asking you, Travis. What should I be doing?"

"If you don't know, isn't it going to be pretty difficult to get other people on board?"

There was an analogy in there somewhere, about people not having to know where a boat was headed to know that they needed to be on it. "Yeah. I see your point. I really have no clue what I'm doing, do I?"

"Jo, you keep asking me questions that I think you should be asking yourself."

"Because you've been there. You are there. You have a life mission, a path."

"Nobody else can tell you your mission, Jo."

"I know. I just . . . I see this need in the community. These women who don't seem to have

29

the connections they need to make their lives better, and I want to help."

"Why you?"

"Now *you're* asking me questions I should be asking myself." She smiled shyly up at him.

He laughed and nodded. "Got me."

I wish. She sighed. Even with her heart and mind laboring full steam to try to flesh out her plans for helping others, there was still a part of Jo that wondered how Travis felt about her. That wanted some hint of where their relationship was going. If they even *had* a relationship.

"The point is, it's not enough to know what you want, Jo. You have to give some thought to how *you* can best serve the needs you see around you. What unique gifts do you bring to the table?"

You tell me. She pressed her lips together to keep herself from fishing for some kind of insight about how Travis felt about her.

"You have to examine your own motivations. Who are you doing this for? Do you really want to serve others or are you trying to make yourself feel better, serving your own interests?"

Ouch! That told her a little bit more of what he thought of her than she had reckoned on.

Jo took a step backward, then looked down to watch the impression of her feet in the wet white sand fill with the incoming tide then disappear as though she had never been there at all.

She could not think of a more apt metaphor for herself. *The girl who has walked in everybody else's shoes trying to keep them happy for so long that now she no longer even leaves a footprint of her own.*

A bleak heaviness descended over her shoulders and chest. She breathed, but only shallow breaths. She fought back the ridiculous urge to burst out crying.

She cleared her throat and raised her head. In doing so she caught a glimpse of Moxie's old truck in the strip of parking spaces along the edge of the beach. That served as a stark reminder of her past, of her family's past, and what she had drawn from it.

Cromwell women did not cry.

Crying was self-indulgent. It did not make things better.

But then what had Jo ever done in her life that made anything better for anyone?

She couldn't think of a single thing.

She had thought she was doing so when she became a Realtor. Helping people find a home, build toward their dreams. But before long she had been sucked into the cycle of buying and selling and winning awards and being the most sought-after name in the business. It became about flipping houses at higher and higher risk for bigger and bigger profit in order to please her boss. And when the risk got too big? Her boss took the profit and left her in a financial mess that even now she had no idea how to dig out of.

Be sweet?

Life so far had neither prepared her nor rewarded her for that.

She glanced at Moxie waving at someone she knew in the lot, walking with her head as high as any fashion model's even while wearing a baseball cap, rolled-up pants and flip-flops.

Be a sister?

Be the lesser of three sisters was more like it.

Be substantial?

A woman that left no footprints for anyone to see, much less follow?

Be a servant of God?

She looked at Travis. So many questions. So many things she simply had no answer for.

Be safe?

That elusive feeling she had never really known, not as a child, not at her chosen field of work, not in her newest relationship.

How could she be any of those things, much less all of them? Jo hadn't even figured out how to be herself.

Finally she looked Travis in the eye, even as Moxie drew closer, and laid it all out for him as earnestly as she could. "What if I ask myself those questions . . . and I don't have the answers?"

"Then you have a lot of work ahead of you

finding them," he told her softly. Another squeeze of her shoulder and a nod to approaching Moxie then he turned and headed back toward the chapel.

Cromwell women do not cry. Jo straightened her back and turned to meet her younger sister.

"Where's he going?"

"I think he's giving me some . . . space."

"Oh?" It was only one syllable but Moxie packed a lot of concern in it.

Jo shook her head. "Apparently I have a lot of work to do."

"Okay. I'm here to help." Moxie patted the canvas bag slung over her shoulder the way a gunslinger might lay a hand lightly on his holster to make sure everyone present knew he hadn't arrived empty-handed. "We the first ones here for the Bible study or, uh, whatever?"

"We're the only ones here." Jo held out her hands to show she had come unarmed, as far as bringing her Bible or any study materials were concerned. The sandals she had removed when she decided to pass the time waiting for her sister by walking along the beach dangled from her fingers. "I had originally asked you to come over hoping you'd come help me convince Travis of the need for this kind of thing."

"*What* kind of thing?" Moxie asked.

"That's part of the work I need to do, to come up with a plan or a mission or . . . I don't know."

Jo felt a little silly. No, she felt a *lot* silly. Travis was right, maybe she had come at this with good intentions but little else. "At least I have a name. I thought we'd call ourselves the Barefoot Believers."

"The what?" Moxie lifted one foot and shook the sand from the sole of her flip-flop.

"It symbolizes humility and a sense of . . . equality. You know the kind of group where you don't feel you have to have the right clothes . . . or the right shoes . . . or any shoes at all, to feel comfortable."

"Comfortable doing what?"

"I don't know." Jo slipped the straps of her sandals down to her wrist and used her free hand to sweep back the coarse blond curls from the back of her neck and sides of her face. "To be like Travis, for example."

"You want to be *like* Travis or you want to be liked *by* Travis?" Moxie's eyes, so familiar and yet so enigmatic, flashed in a teasing challenge.

"Nothing wrong with wanting to be like Travis." Jo stood her ground. "He's accomplished. He's focused. He's substantial."

"Not to mention gorgeous." Moxie feigned a big ol' goofy, doe-eyed sigh. "Except, of course, to me. He's too . . ." She crinkled up her nose. "Too *beachy* for me."

"What's *that* supposed to mean?" Jo snapped.

"You know, sun-kissed hair, cloudproof outlook." Moxie waved her hands around as she spoke. "Too tan, too relaxed—"

"So you'd prefer someone pale and tense?" Jo blurted out in a tone that was neither sweet nor sisterly and entirely too defensive of a man who had yet to make his intentions toward her clear. "Is that what you see in Dr. Lionel Lloyd? You have a marked preference for pasty nervous types?"

"Tan or pale, that doesn't matter." Moxie took it all in stride. "I've had enough of that 'when the going gets tough the tanned go fishing' beach-attitude growing up with my dad, thank you very much."

"I thought the quote was 'when the going gets tough the Weatherbys go fishing.'" Jo cocked her head.

"That's exactly what I'm talking about," Moxie agreed. "Travis Brandt is just a cuter, cooler, Christian-ier version of my dad."

Jo opened her mouth to protest, not because she *knew* it to be a misrepresentation but because she *wanted* it to be with all her heart—especially when a vision popped in her head of Travis with a gut, a hat and a parrot feather.

Moxie forged on before Jo could get out a word. "Tense, I can do without, but I don't know, more *intense?* I could give that a whirl, I suppose."

"Intense? Not a term I'd use for Lionel." Jo

frowned then whispered, "Fits Travis, though."

Accomplished. Focused. Substantial. Beachy but intense. Jo wanted to know what she had been thinking when she believed she could be more like him.

That was a notion she had best give up—go back to her original thought. Sweetness. Sisterly-ness. Being who her mother wanted her to be. Right?

She wished she could talk to either of her sisters about her feelings, lay out her fears and reservations, be truly and fully honest for once in her life, but . . .

"Hmm. How to describe Lionel." Moxie tapped her chin with one finger.

But . . . when everything you attempt ends in embarrassment, indifference or big, fat failure, you always keep your guard up and you never *ever* really feel safe.

"Safe." Jo Cromwell couldn't even begin to imagine what that felt like.

"Yes! Safe," Moxie agreed. "Now there's the perfect word for Lionel."

Jo blinked, trying to make sense of the comment, but she couldn't seem to let go of the subject of her own insecurities. How she questioned each and every single choice she made. Walked away from an encounter only to go over it in her head again and again. She tried her best. She gave her all. Yet that twisting, hot-cheeked angst

36

always came back no matter how much of herself she put into anything, because coming from her it would be nearly worthless.

Not to feel those things pressing in on you day in and day out must be one of the best kinds of freedom in the world, she thought. Like . . .

She closed her eyes and lifted her face to draw in the smells of Florida's Emerald Coast—the salty surf, sun-warmed skin and SPF 30. Yes, even in mid-November the scent of the protective lotion still lingered in the beach air.

A gull cried out.

Foamy water bathed her bare feet then retreated.

Being safe must feel like being a wave.

Or the wind.

Or a bird.

Or anything but a thirty-five-year-old failed perfectionist, buried in business debt, trying to keep the peace in a family where she had always been the kid nobody wanted.

"Jo? Jo? Where are you, girl?" Moxie put her hand on her sister's shoulder.

"Where I am doesn't seem nearly as important as where I am going."

Moxie stepped in close. "Where *are* you going? Wasn't there something you wanted from me, something to do with forming this group of yours? What do you want to do?"

Just once, she thought in a prayer she secretly

suspected even God would dismiss, *I want to do something . . .*

She gazed at the ocean so vast and blue that if you squinted at the horizon you couldn't tell for sure where it left off and the sky began. She thought of pirates and maidens and missionaries both of long ago and of the very modern variety.

She thought of her sisters and their mother, and how much healing they still had to do before they could truly be a family again.

Jo twisted around to look back at the Traveler's Wayside Chapel.

She thought of Travis and how, at the height of his career as a nationally recognized sports announcer, he had walked away from the trappings of fame and money to become a minister at a broken-down chapel in the nearly forgotten former tourist town of Santa Sofia, Florida.

And Jo?

Just once, Lord, I would like to do something right. Something good. Something that makes a difference. Jo held her breath for a moment wondering if she had it in her to say aloud what she longed for more than anything, including her desperate need not to be taken for a fool.

"I am going . . ." She looked at Moxie then at the sand where her own footprints had once been.

It all became clear in that instant.

Her life so far was not working. It was not

serving the Lord. To do that she would have to step out in faith.

She would never be able to make a difference until she started doing something different.

"I am going to the chapel to help clean up after the free meals."

"Okay, I can do that with you." Moxie took a step, leaving her mark on the beach behind her.

"No." Jo put her hand on her sister's arm. "I'm sorry I got you out here today, but I just realized I need to do this alone."

Jo looked at the chapel, the sea, the sand, her sister and made that step she felt sure would lead her in a new direction, a path she would follow for the rest of her life. And all she had to do was trust God and . . .

"Do what?" Moxie asked, a ball cap hiding any emotion in her eyes. "What do you have to do alone, Jo?"

"I have to stop playing it safe."

Chapter Three

Stop playing it safe.

Driving away from the beach, Moxie could not get Jo's words out of her mind.

Not because Moxie needed the same advice.

Far from it!

Moxie wouldn't even know where to begin to play things safe. She'd been practically on her own since the summer when she was sixteen and her foster mother ran off and Billy J began the practice of going fishing whenever things got rough for him.

Moxie gripped the steering wheel of her vintage pickup truck, not sure of which way to turn on the upcoming street. She'd already wasted the morning meeting everyone for breakfast at the cottage so they could share the big newspaper article. Then taken time off from her work schedule to meet Jo only to be sent packing with her Bible in her book bag and her proverbial tail between her legs.

If Moxie merely "worked in property management," as R. Hunt Diamante reported, rather than actually buying, restoring and renting out her own properties, she'd probably have lost her job by now.

She certainly felt as though she was on the verge of losing her patience, if not something more precious. Herself.

Who was she, anyway? Moxie Weatherby or Molly Christina Cromwell? Or some combination of the two? Molly Moxie Christina Cromwell Weatherby? And maybe someday . . . maybe, just maybe she'd add Lloyd to the mess?

"Um, *mix*." She scolded herself for the errant thought. "Add to the mix."

No. Mess was probably a more apt description, if not of who she was, then of who she felt herself slowly becoming. A big, overcrowded mess of expectations and obligations. The truth was that Moxie didn't know who she was or where she belonged or what her future held.

Nothing about her life was, or ever had been, written in stone or inked on legal documents or even scribbled on a wall in permanent marker.

Impermanence.

She had always thought it was the thing that made her independent, which made her successful and, in a way, made her a better Christian.

Now she felt it put to the test. Not whether she had faith or not, but how that faith would manifest in all these new relationships and situations. How could she go from being just Moxie to

41

being a daughter and sister and, in time, a wife?

She shut her eyes to block out at least one of the choices that lay before her—which way to turn.

She didn't recall ever having felt this lost and anxious before. Her foster parents' choices had forced her early in life to become the self-sufficient worker bee that everyone counted on. Now her newly reformed family was pressing in on her so close she wondered that she didn't break out in hives.

If she were the kind to play things safe, she'd turn off her cell phone and go someplace and hide.

"Hey, Mox!" A car pulled up beside her truck, the passenger calling out of the open window at her. "Saw your picture in the paper! Who is that Maxine they mentioned? Another long-lost sister?"

Not that there was any place in Santa Sofia Moxie *could* hide.

"Very funny," Moxie called back, offering a weak smile.

No, she'd never find a place to hide now, not since that story had hit the paper. Everywhere she'd go someone would want to comment on it or ask for *her* comments about it, for sure.

"You should go introduce yourself to that new editor, make him print your name right," the off-duty waitress called as the car pulled out and turned left, toward town.

"Ri-i-i-i-ght. I may just do that." *When pigs fly.* She gave a cheery wave and flipped on her right turn blinker.

Maybe she'd go out to the Bait Shack. After all, it was nearing lunchtime and her dad would ask her to pitch in and wait tables. Or walk around with a pitcher and give refills of sweet tea. Or worst of all, tag along with him and Dodie while they took the fishing boat out for the afternoon. The pair, who had become fast friends, would fill the hours talking about the thing that had made them bond so quickly—her.

She flipped her blinker off and put her forehead against the wheel.

She could go see the so-called love of her life. So called by everyone, including the good doctor himself, but Moxie. Did she really love Lionel Lloyd? She thought she did. She *liked* him.

But not enough to want to go have lunch with him on what was shaping up to be a really rotten day.

Love was too hard a concept to tackle right now. Love in all its forms seemed to be at the root of most of her frustrations. Not just for Lionel but for her sisters and her mother . . . her *mothers,* plural.

Yes, her foster mother had deserted her, leaving behind a lot of pain, confusion and an entirely inadequate note: "Isn't there something better than this?" But that didn't make her any less the woman who had taken Moxie in as a young girl and helped raise her to her teens.

Was getting involved with Dodie and her daughters some kind of betrayal to the mother who had done all that for her? Or was trusting anyone to play the role of mom a betrayal to the woman Moxie felt she had formed of herself all on her own?

Moxie looked left, then right.

What to do? Where to go?

She loved the once-bustling tourist town of little Santa Sofia, Florida. She loved that she could spend her mornings at the beach and her nights under a covering of stars so thick they seemed more plentiful than wildflowers in a meadow. She loved the life she had made for herself here in no small part because of the lives her work allowed her to touch. Because she had a hand in fixing up and preserving so many of the houses and buildings all around town, she wasn't just a "part" of the community, her contributions wove through it, block by block, home by home, person by person.

Now she didn't know where to turn. Not in her life, not in her relationships, not on the very roads of the town she loved.

She raised her eyes and immediately saw the slender stack of business cards she kept secured by a rubber band to the sun visor of her truck.

Weatherby Property Management, Inc.
M. Weatherby
My house is your home.

Moxie meant that. Despite the reckless dismissal of her contributions—and not even getting her name right—in print by the R. Hunt Diamante fellow, what Moxie did mattered to her. She made a difference in people's lives. Because of that, she felt she made Santa Sofia a better place to live.

Another car roared up behind her.

She put her head down again and groaned, bracing herself for the inevitable calling out from the passing driver about the article.

She clenched her teeth.

For someone physically alone in her own truck, raised to feel that in the whole wide world she could only count on herself, Moxie felt crowded into a place so small she could hardly think. But the one thought she could manage was that if she wanted all this new family–old life business to work, she was going to have to do as Jo had advised, stop playing it safe.

That meant setting boundaries.

"Boundaries," she whispered, liking even the sound of the word.

She'd start with her dad.

She raised her head slightly. "No more working for free each and every time I walk into the Bait Shack."

Then Dodie.

Her eyes peered over the dash to the parting of the road ahead. No more expecting Moxie to call her Mom or behave like the little long-lost Molly Christina of Dodie's expectations.

Then Jo and Kate.

She poked her nose over the rim of the steering wheel. "They'll take it best of all." Of course, they really didn't need anything more than a gentle reminder that Moxie needed time to get used to her new it's-a-sisterhood-not-a-competition status.

Then . . .

She lifted her chin, pushed her shoulders back. "Then I just might head down to that newspaper office and make sure that new editor never gets my name wrong again."

And then . . .

And then the honking began.

Moxie just about leaped out of her seat.

"Who in Santa Sofia honks?" That was the kind of behavior they occasionally got during the peak of tourist season but not in November. "And at *me?*"

Everyone knew her truck and they knew if it wasn't moving, it had either broken down or she had! That is, she had had a breakdown in communications most likely with her dad, but maybe with a client or contractor. Everyone in town knew this meant she was stuck on her cell phone and might be sitting there awhile. So people had gotten used to just rolling on around her.

Moxie checked her rearview mirror. Sure enough, she recognized neither the white muscle-car convertible with the tan leather interior—a car like that she could have remembered—nor the man sitting behind the wheel. Correction, the man *seething* behind the wheel.

He honked again and said something that she couldn't quite make out, for which she suspected she should be grateful.

His black hair was clipped so short she wondered if he'd recently shaved it all off and this was a couple weeks' growth. His complexion wasn't pale by any means but definitely not tanned. Someone who spent far more time indoors than your average Floridian, she decided on the spot. He had on sunglasses that wrapped around his face like some superhero's mask, only the black frames and lenses made it impossible to see his eyes. And a patch of beard that she supposed was meant to make him look hip or cool or whatever word people not stuck in a small town like her would use to describe themselves.

But she couldn't help thinking it made him look like the paper cutout of the Pharaoh they stuck on the felt board to act out the story of Moses in Sunday school.

That Pharaoh was one bad dude. A loner type. Someone unaccustomed to things not going his way. A guy who didn't play well with others.

Moxie's stomach tightened. She thought of rolling down the window and yelling for him to go around her.

Before she could, the man got out of his car.

She gasped.

Santa Sofians did not get out of their cars to express dissatisfaction with another driver's behavior. They drove up and hollered about it like civilized people. This did not feel right.

She put her hand on the door handle. She'd just pop it open and assuage this stranger with the old Southern custom of slopping sugar. That meant she'd apologize and fret, and flirt and compliment relentlessly until the man either surrendered to her charm or got sick of it all and did what he should have done in the first place. Skedaddled on past her.

That's when she noticed his hand clenching and unclenching; there were black smudges on his long fingers and fresh cuts across his knuckles.

All thoughts of charm and sugar deserted her then and all she could think was that Santa Sofia was about to experience its very first case of road rage. And when they wrote the story of her untimely demise in the *Sun Times*, that doofus of a new editor probably still wouldn't get her name right.

No way was she sitting still for that. The road rage, not the name thing.

She promised herself then and there not to let little things like mistakes in their tiny town paper get to her ever again, if she could only get out of this unscathed.

She revved the engine.

The guy stopped in the road.

The truck lurched forward and she prayed it wouldn't stall as she flipped on her left blinker and then spun the wheel hard to the right. She high-tailed it toward Billy J's Bait Shack Seafood Buffet.

As she drove she frowned and glanced at the Bible in the bag beside her and then at her business cards. All right, she did have a little of Jo in her. She had a little of the desire to please others. And given the choice between leading a strange man to someplace where there might not be anyone around to protect her and a public place where there would probably already be a couple local cops and also an arsenal of things she could pull from the wall—from fishing nets to a varnished swordfish—to defend herself, she'd choose the safest bet. She did play it safe more than she liked to admit.

But that did not discount the boundary thing.

In fact, the Road Rage Pharaoh Wannabe had helped cement the idea in her mind.

Now there was a man who knew what he

wanted and did not hesitate to let others know what he would or would not stand for.

Moxie could do that. She could let people know that she wouldn't let them keep her from making her own way in the world. She could make it clear that she wouldn't let them hold her up or waste her time any longer.

She would be much more polite about expressing herself than the masked honker, of course. She'd be calmer. Kinder. Ditch the intimidation and loud repetitive noises angle altogether.

Unless she absolutely had to resort to those things to get her father's or Dodie's attention, then . . . Well, she'd do what she had to do, and playing it safe would not even be a consideration.

Chapter Four

"Vince! Am I ever glad to see you here." Moxie slid in next to her sister Kate's onetime fiancé, Vince Merchant.

She scooted in close to him, then closer, hunkering down to use his broad shoulders and general above-average height for cover. Not that she thought it would do much good. If only the man had chosen one of the booths along the outside of the main dining floor instead of taking a seat on a communal bench at the long row of tables at the center of the large room. Sure, she'd have found herself up against a huge plate-glass window—every booth in Billy J's was under a huge plate-glass window—but she could have compensated by scrunching down and getting lost between the dark, highly varnished wood paneling and the dark, highly varnished table.

Everything in Billy J's was highly varnished, from the booths to the scattering of individual table-and-chair sets to the two long rows of plank-like picnic-style tables and matching benches that stretched the length of the dining floor. Varnish, her father said, made everything easier to clean. Moxie suspected that meant it hid the dirt. Also, she reasoned that when everything around you glinted with varnish it didn't make the food, most all of it glistening with grease, seem so unnatural.

The local fire department made Billy J's Bait Shack Seafood Buffet post a sign saying the place had a maximum occupancy of 203. During tourist season it pretty much stayed at full capacity with an overflow crowd that gathered out front, often bringing lawn chairs to make themselves comfortable for the long wait. At almost 1:00 p.m. on this November day it was practically deserted by those standards. Though to the inexperienced onlooker it still would have seemed to have drawn a pretty healthy crowd. Healthy being a subjective term, given that everything they served had been battered and fried, even the vegetables, and the food always came with bucket-size soft drinks.

Still, Moxie counted herself blessed to have found a friendly face in the diminished crowd.

"You don't have to duck." Vince scooted away to give them both some elbow room. "Your dad isn't here to press you into service today."

"I'm not avoiding my dad," she whispered emphatically then felt compelled to add, "Today."

"Oh, yeah?" The simple question practically demanded to know just who she was avoiding, and implied that he suspected it might be another member of her suddenly expanded family.

Moxie had known Vince since, as her dad might say, Moses was in knee britches. Well, maybe not quite that long, but for just over half of her thirty years. So it seemed to her as though he'd always been a fixture in Santa Sofia, and in her life. Anyway, she already regarded the man as something of a brother, not a big brother, mind you, even though she was closer in age to his son than to the man himself. No, Moxie felt toward Vince, much as she did to her father, like the adult in the relationship.

Not that Vince was immature. He just had this soft spot for his only son that made him . . . well, made Moxie feel like she wanted to flick the man on the ear and tell him to grow up and get a life of his own instead of trying to keep his son in a state of perpetual dependency.

In other words, no way was Moxie going to allow Vince to talk to her like that. "Oh, yeah? Don't try to play that game with me, Merchant."

"Game? Me? You're the one who ran in here like someone playing cops and robbers, then ducked behind me like . . ." He scrubbed his blunt fingertips over his bristled jaw and frowned. "Why are you ducking behind me?"

"Ugh." She sat up at last, satisfied the man hadn't followed her and wasn't about to come roaring through the door. "It's a long story."

"It's an all-you-can-eat buffet." He folded his arms over the table. "I have time."

"I just think, or *thought,* really, that maybe someone . . ." She met Vince's amused and a bit annoyed gaze and realized if she wanted him to take her seriously, she would have to spell it out for him. "Just listen up. Somebody followed me here. I *thought* somebody followed me here!"

"Why didn't you say so?" He turned his attention to his food, obviously unimpressed with that bit of news. "Who?"

"Who?" Somehow blurting out she feared that Road Rage Pharaoh was on her trail didn't seem like a great way to get him to take her more seriously. So Moxie shrugged a little and mumbled, "No one. Well, no one you know."

"Hmm. No one I know. That rules out everyone in town, most especially your sisters." He grinned.

"It's silly, I suppose. Just . . . well . . . it started when I kind of stopped at a stop sign."

"You stopped? At a stop sign? Aren't you supposed to do that?"

"Yeah. I just didn't start back up again."

"Truck trouble?" Again. He didn't add that part but it was there, further evidence to Moxie that nobody in town would make a big deal out of her stopping overly long on the road.

"No, not truck trouble, this time. More like . . ." She pressed her lips together then looked at

Vince. Of all the people she knew, he would understand her issues over the return of the Cromwells better than anyone. "More like family trouble."

Vince chuckled then paused and frowned. "Everyone healthy?"

"Well, I guess *healthy* is a relative term." She opened her mouth to say more, then suddenly put together what she said, laughed at her unintentional pun and finally relaxed just a little. "*Relative* term. That's a good one."

"Maybe I should rephrase that question. Are *you* okay?"

"Yeah, I'm fine. Everyone is fine as far as I know. It was more one of *those* moments, you know?"

He shook his head.

"You know, *those* moments," she insisted as if saying it with a little extra emphasis would make the lightbulb go off in his head. "When everything going on in your life crashes in on you and you just . . ."

"Deal with it?" he suggested.

Moxie huffed in exasperation. "This kind of thing is easier for you because you're . . . you know . . ."

"A genius?"

"A dad. You know, you have a family. I've only had my foster folks. One of which was never really all that involved and the other was, well—"

she raised her hands to offer their very surroundings as evidence of her point "—my dad."

"Hmm." Meaning *I don't have the slightest idea what you are talking about.*

"This trying to make things work while considering your whole family. What *they* want. What *they* need. Then taking into account how much you have to spare emotionally, physically and still have a life of your own." She put her elbows on the table and rested her forehead in her hands. "It's all so new to me."

"And that made your truck stall?"

"No. It made my *brain* overheat." She shut her eyes. That didn't quite describe it, either. "Or maybe it was my heart? Anyway, the results were the same—I feel like I'm not getting anywhere."

"*That* I understand!" He pinched the bridge of his nose.

She wanted to ask if he had a headache. He looked as though he had a whopper. But she feared he would not only say yes, but then accuse her of giving it to him.

"Don't sweat it, Vince. I'll work it all out." She looked across the room at the faded photo on the wall of Dodie holding her as a child and sighed.

Vince followed her line of vision then shook his head and gave her a pat on the back. "My advice is don't borrow trouble. Don't let yourself get all worked up about this stuff. Keep some time for yourself. Have some places where you can escape, where you don't have to even think about your family."

"In Santa Sofia?" She gave him one of those looks. "Besides, no matter where I go, my family, it seems, is the type that even when they are nowhere near you, they are right there *with* you. You know what I mean?"

"Yeah. I guess that's something about family that I take for granted. I feel that my son and granddaughter and, by extension, my daughter-in-law and now Kate, are always with me, always a part of me."

Moxie nodded to show her sympathy.

Vince broke into a slow, wistful smile. "I like that."

"Well, I don't. At least, I don't know if I like it or not, but since neither they nor I seem to be going anywhere—"

"And the story finally comes full circle."

"What?"

"You started this rant by telling me your truck had stalled at a stopsign and something happened."

"It didn't stall. *I* did." She rested her forehead in her hands again. If she hadn't given Vince a headache, she sure was well on her way to giving herself one. "I was sitting there, thinking. And everybody just went around me, you know, the way you do when you see my truck stopped."

"Sure."

"Except for this one guy."

"Who?"

She pressed her lips together to keep the name Road Rage Pharaoh from tumbling out. "I, um, I didn't recognize him. The point is that he got out of his car and started right for me."

"What did he want?"

"Want? I don't know what he wanted." She swung her leg over the bench. If the guy had truly followed her, he'd have burst through the doors by now. "I took off. Used my head about it if I say so myself."

"Yeah?"

"Put on my blinker then went the opposite direction. I drove down alleys and backtracked, anything I could to lose him."

"And he was tailing you this whole time?"

"No. I mean, I don't know. I just wanted to make sure he *couldn't*."

"Yeah, because that 'left turn signal, big noisy vintage truck roaring around the corner to the right' ploy fools even the most heinous bad guys every time."

"I didn't say he was heinous." Actually he was kind of cute. "He got out of his car, after all."

"Maybe he thought you needed help." He stuck his fork into a mound of coleslaw and muttered, "In more ways than one."

"Very funny." She stood, her eyes narrowed at the man she had thought she could rely upon for cover. "Thanks anyway for your concern. That'll teach me to be more careful who I seek out whenever—"

"Whenever it's convenient or necessary for you?" He tipped his head and caught her off guard with an earnest, unyielding glare.

"What?"

"You've spent the past few minutes telling me how hard you've got it with your new sisters and Dodie closing in on you. All the while wasn't that exactly what you were doing to me?"

"I came to you because I was scared, Vince."

"And you think your sisters and your mom aren't scared by all that's happened? By the possibility that everything they've prayed for all their lives might blow up in their faces?"

"I . . . uh . . ." Dodie, Kate and Jo always seemed so confident. A team. The ones in control of everything. Of every*one*.

"Think about it." He went back to his meal. "It might just create a little more room in your world."

"Room? My . . . ?" How could he say something like that to her? Something so penetrating. Something so guilt-inducing. Something so true. How could he say that, then go back to stuffing popcorn shrimp into his mouth as if he had washed his hands of the whole thing?

59

He stuck the pad of his thumb into his mouth to clean off deep-fried shrimp grease and his eyes met hers. "You need anything else?"

She needed to scream. She needed to stand there in the heart of the Bait Shack and pitch a wall-eyed, no-holds-barred hissy fit. She needed—

"Doesn't anyone in this town grasp the concept of moving on?" She heard the masculine voice, complete with the smarmy Yankee accent and attitude to match, just seconds before the tray jabbed her in the back.

For an instant she thought of letting loose on the poor man and taking out all her frustrations but one glance at Vince told her he'd get far too much fun out of watching that. So she decided with a split-second's notice to do that slopping sugar thing she had hoped to use on the man in the white muscle car. She'd be so friendly and flirtatious, so sweet and so decidedly Southern that the man would find himself helpless to do anything but . . .

She turned. "Call the police! This is the man who followed me!"

"That seems highly unlikely since not only was this the place I was headed to from the moment I left my office but also since I got here before you." He held up his tray of food as evidence of how long he'd been in the place and just what he had come for, then took a step as if to go around her and forward.

"I was raised here. It is not possible for you to have gotten here before me."

He stared at her for a moment then looked away and groaned. "You're the woman who was blocking the road."

"I wasn't blocking anything. You could have gone around me. Other people went around me."

"Other people?" He tipped his head as if he had to think about that a moment. "Had to go around you? Is that like a thing with you? You have issues sharing space with, oh, say, the rest of the people on the planet?"

Vince snickered.

Moxie tensed. Any other day if the man had asked any other question she'd have backed down. Moxie talked a big game in her head but, mostly, she backed down. That's why her bold and brassy new family's, well, boldness and brassiness had such an effect on her. She didn't have the wherewithal to stand up to them. To stand up for herself.

Stop playing it safe. Jo's words came back to her.

Moxie had promised herself she would set boundaries and she didn't see any reason not to start with this stranger barging in on her home turf demanding she be the one to move aside.

He took a step.

She blocked him.

61

He stepped to the side away from where she had moved.

She followed suit. When this kind of thing happened accidentally in the narrow passages between these tables, someone—usually Billy J himself—would holler out, "Hey, no dancing on the dining floor, we're a wholesome establishment, y'all!" Today, no one said a word.

But everybody watched.

They probably made quite a sight, too. Moxie with her cap and flip-flops looking like a fresh-faced surfer girl who wasn't afraid of the big waves or an overgrown bossy boy. Only this wasn't a *boy*.

One look at him told anyone with eyes that the man who had jangled her down to her very last nerve was all man. Older than her, but not by much. Taller, too. Just a few inches, not enough to make it difficult for her to hold his gaze with hers.

His dark gaze. His deep gaze. His "sleepy-lidded, superconfident but just might break into a smile that would make his brown eyes sparkle" gaze.

Moxie wavered.

He started to step around her again.

She rallied back to reality and cut him off.

He sighed. "If you'll just step aside, I'd like to find a seat before my arteries close up from sheer proximity to this stuff."

"I don't think so." She meant she wasn't stepping aside, but if he took it as a staunch defense of her daddy's fine food fare, then so be it.

"Okay, I guess here is as good a place as any to get a jump start on my first heart attack." He slid onto the bench directly across from Vince.

Directly over the boundary she had just tried to set. "Hey! No way. Uh-uh. Don't even try to sit there, buddy."

"Too late. Not only have I tried it. I have succeeded." He snapped his napkin and laid it across his knees.

"Oh, no. No." She started to reach for the white paper resting on top of the faded denim of his jeans, then caught herself. "You can't stay here."

"Who says I can't?"

"I do!" She put her hand on her chest. "*I* say you can't."

"And you are?"

"The person about this close to calling the police to have you forcibly removed from this place."

"Hmm." He nodded at her then shook his head slightly, the way a dog shakes his head to get rid of slobber. Then he calmly fixed his gaze on Vince and offered another instinctive reaction without regard to who might be present to suffer the consequences. He tossed off that look that all males seem capable of when they think a female is doing something irrational, ridiculous or, well, typically female.

63

Vince recognized it right away. He must have, because he extended his hand in a show of instant kinship and said, "Vince Merchant. Feel free to sit and eat as much as you can in peace before the cops show up."

"Don't fraternize with him, Vince. He's, like, the enemy. The . . . the . . . interloper. The . . . the . . ."

"New editor of the *Santa Sofia Sun Times*." The man grasped Vince's hand and gave it a firm shake, but those dark eyes, dancing with amusement, focused solely on her as he said, "R. Hunt Diamante."

"You . . . are?" Moxie sank down to sit on the bench again, a little stunned.

"Almost nobody actually calls me 'R.' " He grinned.

A totally gorgeous, I-know-I-have-the-upper-hand kind of grin that, despite the sheer cockiness of it, still charmed her enough that she could hardly form a complete thought, much less sentence.

Her stalker, Road Rage Pharaoh, this adorable man with the mesmerizing eyes, they were all the same guy. R. Hunt Diamante. The new editor. The guy who called her Maxine! The man she was going to give her card and a piece of her mind.

Just that fast she snapped to her senses, pulled her shoulders up and stabbed her finger in his direction. "You are just the guy I am looking for."

Chapter Five

"May not be much of a journalist, but you've got to respect his style." Vince chuckled softly as he leaned against the doorway of her mostly empty office in the Urgent Care Clinic. He'd come by a little early to pick up Kate from her shift and had invited her to dinner.

Though she had closed her practice in Atlanta, signed the contracts and written the check to make herself a partner in the lone emergency medical facility in town, Kate had not started to work at the place full-time. With possible surgeries pending, it seemed best to only keep part-time hours for a while. So she just filled in now and then for Lionel or the residents from the hospital in nearby Waverly, earning a few extra bucks.

"You should have seen the look on Moxie's face." Vince shook his head, still smiling. "I love your little sister like, well, a little sister, but when she gets worked up over something—or worked up over almost nothing at all, like today —she is her father's daughter. Billy J's daughter, I mean."

Kate nodded. *Moxie. Sister. Billy J.* She pretended it all registered, when in fact she used the time he was talking to study the deep lines fanning out from the corners of Vince's compelling eyes.

She had seen the beginnings of those lines nearly twenty years ago when they had first fallen in love. She found it funny in a not-laugh-out-loud, not-quite-peculiar way to see the way time had treated the man without the benefit of experiencing all that time with him. It had the effect of a before-and-after photo, or maybe more like when a favorite old TV show from childhood gathered the "old gang" for a reunion show.

She hated those shows. She hated the idea of having lost out on so much time then being expected to pick up and care about those characters again as if they had always been there in TV Land going on with their lives. But she fell for it every time. Probably because it was the one thing she wanted most in her own life—a second chance to get it right.

"Kate?"

"Hmm." She shook her head. Hearing her name snapped her back to the present. The conversation replayed quickly in her mind. Vince had told her a story about Moxie and the Bait Shack because . . . "We're not eating at the Bait Shack tonight, are we?"

"What gave you that idea? Oh!" He laughed again. "No. No, no Bait Shack tonight. Tonight we're having dinner someplace very special."

"Oh?" *Dinner? Special?* A mental red flag went up. If this were one of those cheesy reunion shows, that would mean *something*. That would mean something in the very most meaningful of ways, she thought to herself in her old reliable Scat-Kat Katie way, careful to avoid even the hint of a mention of possible commitment and the prospect of making a future together. "That's nice."

Pause. Remain poised. Don't read too much into this. She fussed with a stack of forms on her desk before looking up at him again and trying to sound totally devoid of any expectation as she said, "Where . . ."

Her uncharacteristically high-pitched voice broke. She blushed and cleared her throat, then tried again. "Where do you plan to take me for dinner?"

"Chez Merchant."

She'd been absent from Santa Sofia for a long time but it was a small enough place that she had learned every eatery in it and in Waverly, a town forty miles away, in the two months since her return. She crinkled up her nose. "I don't know that."

"My place?"

"Oh! Your . . . We're eating dinner at your place.

Um, eating *in* at your place. Your house. Your home."

Kate hadn't been to his house. He'd always come up to hers, which made sense, what with Kate's injured foot limiting her mobility and comfort levels. Besides, Vince's son Gentry and his family lived right across the street.

Vince's house. It felt like a big move forward in their relationship. A *good* move. Her stomach did a little flip-flop. She reined in her reaction and went back to shuffling those forms. "Yeah, okay, sounds great."

"Glad you like it."

Another shuffle through. Her whole body tingled with the urge to ask him why he wanted to take her to his home now. Why tonight? And what made it *special?* What she asked instead was, "What's to eat?"

"Uh . . . I hadn't . . . It's a . . . It's a surprise."

"A surprise?" For her or him? He obviously didn't want to tell her so she tried another approach that might give her a clue about the evening. "What inspired this?"

He looked at her as though she had just walked into the conversation. "Your sister."

Kate *felt* as though she'd just walked into the conversation. "Jo?"

"Moxie."

"Moxie told you to have me over for dinner?"

"No, she spoiled my lunch."

"What?"

"The story I just told you? About her showing up at the Bait Shack? Then this Hunt fellow horns in, too? Tells her if she doesn't like his story to write her own? If she wants to talk about it further to see him at his office because he's on lunch break? Any of this ringing a bell?"

"Most of it." She didn't want to admit she'd only been half listening to what he was saying because she'd been too busy admiring the lines in his face, daydreaming about old TV shows and obsessing about whether or not he would ever propose to her again. "But I don't see what it has to do with eating at your place."

"You left out two important words. Eating *in peace* at my place. This relationship between us is so . . ." He raised his hand.

It was a good hand. Calloused and tanned. Rugged and a little scarred, but with short, clean nails that showed his attention to detail. Kate liked those hands. She'd like them better if there was a wedding ring on the third finger of the left one.

Wait.

This relationship between us is so . . .

What? She'd gotten so distracted looking at the man she had lost track of listening to him.

He tilted his raised hand back and forth rather than say more. So, before she could stop herself, she said more. "So *what?* Rocky? Unsteady? Iffy?"

The second the words came out she regretted them and slapped her hand over her mouth as if she could push them back inside and trap them there.

That only made Vince laugh again. Then he shook his head and said, "None of the above, but still, I don't want to leave it open to public scrutiny—and in a town this size, there isn't anywhere to go that's not 'public' or anything better for people to *do* than scrutinize."

She sat back in her seat. "And you think the two of us spending the evening at your house won't set people talking?"

He tapped the side of his head. "I've thought of a way to elevate it above all that."

That piqued her curiosity. An engagement announcement, or that golden wedding band, would both be excellent ways to quell any idle talk. She folded her hands on top of her desk. Cool, collected and coy, she used all her communication skills to say, "Oh?"

His grin broke slowly but spread to include a glint in his eyes and to bring out those laugh lines in full force.

Kate could barely contain herself. The man might just throw his plans out the window and propose right here and now. She pivoted her chair around just in case he wanted to drop to his knee in front of her.

He pushed away from the door frame and took

a step toward her, then said, "We'll have a chaperone."

"A . . . what?" She almost fell forward at that and had to grab the edge of the desk to keep from swiveling herself around to face the back wall.

"A very short chaperone who goes to bed early, and doesn't know enough words to tell everyone in town our business yet."

"Oh." She eased out a long breath and scooted her chair back under the desk. "We're babysitting Fabiola."

"Gentry is dropping her off at six-thirty. They have some kind of dinner with a relative of Esperanza's from Miami. Do you mind?"

An evening at home with Vince and the darling grandchild he adored. It wasn't what she had envisioned, but compared to all the evenings she had spent alone or on dates or business dinners when she couldn't wait to be alone again? "It sounds wonderful. I can't wait."

So maybe she wouldn't have her proposal tonight. It would still be sweet to share an evening of domestic tranquility with Vince. Just the two of them . . . and his grandchild . . . and the great, unspoken, unsettled question that she didn't dare broach and he didn't seem ready to ask hovering in the air all around them.

Oh, yeah, tonight was going to be wonderful indeed.

Chapter Six

Vince's house was small. It had probably once been a vacation home, built as little more than a place to sleep and change and eat, if that eating didn't require any fancy maneuvers or large appliances in the kitchen. It still had that feel to it. As if whoever occupied it had never really made it home. As if, at the end of a long tourist season, or if, given any reason at all to move along, whoever lived in the place could pack up and go in a matter of hours.

Yet Vince had clearly lived here a very long time.

Kate could tell that with just a glance through the living room. The coatrack hung inside the door at the perfect height for Vince to hang his handyman's tool belt when he came home after work. The furniture was clean but worn, a sure sign of a single dad now living alone who did not entertain much.

Then, there was the kitchen. Too small for a larger family to have put up with for very long, the door frame bore the marks of Gentry's growth year by year. Starting at age six.

Kate held her breath for a moment. Six. She'd known him at that age, at the size indicated by the mark on the door frame.

"Did you move into this place just after—" She cut herself off suddenly, embarrassingly aware what she blurted out next might stir up a whole hornets' nest of hard feelings.

"Just after you ran off?" he finished for her.

Ouch. She dipped her head slightly and stared at her paper plate piled with fried samplings from the Bait Shack—Vince's "surprise" dinner arrangements. "I was going to say after we broke up."

"Did we break up, Kate?" He pushed away his own plate, now just picked-over slaw, a corncob and grease stains. He appeared more thoughtful than anything else, but there was an edge to his words that challenged her. "That's not how I remember it."

"We've gone over this before, Vince." She took up his plate and laid it on top of hers, literally signaling an end to the meal and figuratively trying to tell him she had had enough of this conversation.

What was there to talk about anyway?

It had all happened so fast. Over the course of one long summer when Kate had come to stay at her family's summer cottage after college. Vince was older, already a father and widowed since six-year-old Gentry had been an infant.

He doted on the boy then. Still did, and he

indulged and overprotected him. A habit he had only just committed to stop as he now saw it had done the kid more harm than good.

The romance between Kate and Vince had been brief but intense and before the summer had ended not only had Vince proposed but Gentry had begun to look to her as a mother figure.

A mother! Kate? Good ol' Scat-Kat Katie? The girl who had always blamed herself for not telling her mother immediately the night the girl's father had kidnapped baby Moxie? No way. She wasn't ready. Not to make that kind of leap for a relationship so new, so untried.

No, Kate was unprepared to accept the responsibility of marriage and motherhood. She feared her own shortcomings would bring more pain and disappointment to those she loved and that another child, Gentry, would suffer heartbreak and disappointment if she failed. Or rather, if she failed again.

That seemed a lifetime ago. Certainly most of Gentry's lifetime. If only Vince could move past it. If only he could believe how much she had grown.

"I can't keep going over the past. *We* can't. Not if we hope to build any kind of future together."

"We can't fool ourselves and pretend it never happened, either, Kate. I don't know about you but I can't watch every word I say to try to skirt around the truth, and I don't think I can have a relationship where that is a requirement before we can build a future together."

Kate raised her chin, ready to protest that she did not intend for them to skirt around the truth. Then she recalled how they had gotten into this conversation, when she had kept herself from stirring up the past. She bowed her head, shaking it, and laughed at the irony of it all.

"What's so funny?" he asked, his smile tentative but encouraging as he lowered his own head to try to duck down and find her gaze.

"I am," she said. "*This* is."

"Really?"

"No, not really," she admitted. "It's just, you have to laugh sometimes, don't you? At all of this? At how hard we try not to hurt one another's feelings by not bringing up how much we hurt one another's feelings?"

"Did I hurt your feelings, Kate?" He tipped his head to one side as though honestly struggling to remember a specific incident or transgression. "You never told me that before. All those years ago, was it something I said? Something I did?"

"Yes." They had been through this before, but not quite like this. Not in a quiet moment, just the two of them sitting over a dinner table talking like old friends. Talking as if whatever they

75

said would not come between them but was just part of who they were, who they had been, who they hoped to be.

"What, Kate?" He reached out and took her hand in his, turning it over so that the palm rested upward. "What did I say? What did I do?"

"You said you loved me and you asked me to marry you."

"I remember." He stared at her a moment and when she didn't say more he stroked her hand from her wrist to her fingertips then looked her deep in the eyes and asked, "And that hurt your feelings and sent you running?"

"No." She closed her hand and gave his strong fingers a squeeze. "That scared me witless and *that* sent me running."

He held her gaze.

"I sent myself running," she confessed. "I grew up in a family where nothing, not even love, it seemed, was permanent. I'd seen the devastation of a failed marriage and felt the anguish of losing one parent who left and losing a part of the parent who stayed behind."

"You thought our marriage would fail?"

"It all felt so rushed."

"You could have asked me for more time."

"What about Gentry? Could I have asked him for more time? Could I have asked a six-year-old to hold his feelings in check, to not get his hopes up that he'd finally have his dream of a regular family until I was sure things would work out between us?"

Vince looked away at last.

He couldn't argue with that. The man had all but ordered his entire life around taking care of his son. He could not find fault with her for having done the same, no matter how much it had cost them both.

"But that was then." She reached out and took his hand in both of hers. "And Gentry is a grown-up with a baby of his own and I'm—"

"Anyone home? Dad? Your favorite grand-baby is in the house!" Gentry's voice startled them both.

Kate jerked her hands away.

Vince jumped up out of his seat. "We're in the kitchen. Come on in!"

He took a step toward the door, in a hurry to get to his son and grandchild, then paused, turned back, took Kate's hand again and kissed it. "We'll talk about this later, okay?"

It wasn't until she nodded and mouthed "okay" back to him that he let go of her and went through the door and into the living room to greet Gentry and Fabbie.

"Later," she whispered. They would talk later. They would resolve old issues later. He would propose . . . *when?*

"Soon." Kate lifted her eyes to heaven and poured her heart into the simplest and most sincere prayer she could offer. "Please?"

"Look who's here, Fabbie!" Vince came back through the door carrying the dark-haired little girl who called him "Paw-Paw."

"Hi, princess!" Kate gave the girl a wave. She would have liked to have taken the girl in her arms but because of her injured foot, they had all agreed they would teach the baby not to cling to, climb over or be held by Kate for now. It killed Kate, but Vince didn't seem to mind getting to hold the child whenever Kate was around.

To say he adored Fabbie would be totally undervaluing the concept of adoration.

"Hi, Gentry." Kate leaned over and extended her wave to the young man she had, until a couple of months ago, always seen as a kid with big brown eyes, curly hair and a fragile heart she didn't dare break.

"Hey, Kate! If we'd have known Dad planned to drag you into this, we'd have made him come to our house to put less stress on you."

Vince gave his son a nudge. "Having dinner with me at my house hardly qualifies as a stressful event."

"I meant less stress on her foot because we'd just be across the street from her house." Gentry laughed then gave his dad a wary look. "Though now that you mention it, you didn't cook, did you?"

"Bait Shack takeout." Kate lifted the edge of one of the paper plates.

"Ah. Then, yeah, our house would have definitely caused less stress for Kate, for sure." Another look to his dad, this time less wary and more wise to his old man's ways. "We actually have some *real* food in our fridge."

It did her good to see the two of them together, and with little Fabbie grinning in delight between them.

Yes, Vince had mistakenly lived his life for Gentry and she had not helped that by running away instead of staying and dealing with her issues. But she was back now. Vince loved her, and she loved him. They could talk about their past and they would find a way to get beyond it, she just knew it.

"Anyway, I guess it's a good thing you guys are both here." Gentry shifted his weight from one foot to the other. He looked down.

Vince tensed.

But then everything Gentry did seemed to make Vince tense, as though he must stand always at the ready to rush in to the kid's rescue.

Old habits die hard, she supposed.

"There's something I really think I need to tell you about this dinner." When Gentry looked up, he seemed more sure of himself, more determined. He seemed to have grown up a little in those few seconds. "Dad, I, uh, tonight . . . it's not just about dinner. Pera's uncle wants to hire me for a really good job."

Her gaze brushed over the hash marks on the door frame and she smiled. Gentry had become a young man who did not need his dad to bail him out or make excuses for him anymore.

Vince was free to make a real home at last. A home with her, she hoped.

"In Miami," Gentry concluded. "If I take this job, Pera and the baby and I will be leaving Santa Sofia."

Or maybe not, Kate amended as she focused on Vince's stricken expression.

No matter what he had said about letting Gentry live his own life, she could see in that moment that the man had meant that in the context of living his own life within a few miles radius of this tiny little house, in this tiny tourist town, where there was no room for her, much less for the home she hoped to build with Vince here.

Chapter Seven

"It happened again." Travis looked up. He smiled as he stretched his arms out, then up, then bent them in order to lace his hands behind his head.

Jo paused in the doorway to soak it all in. The awesome sight of the overworked, underpaid minister in his natural element, his office. "*What* happened again?"

"The *Sun Times* got something wrong."

She crossed the threshold and craned her neck to try to catch a glimpse of the paper strewn over his beat-up, army-surplus, metal desk. "They ran another article about my family?"

"Nope." He sat up and splayed one large suntanned hand over the open pages and gave them a twist so she could easily read along as he said, "Check out their weather forecast, though."

She peered at the row of small cartoonish drawings depicting the expectations for each day of the week. "I don't—"

"See, right there for today?" He jabbed his finger on the picture. "Cloudy with no chance of sunshine."

Jo tipped her head to one side, confused.

"And yet in you walk and my whole day is brighter."

Jo responded to the sweet but corny line with an exaggerated roll of her eyes. Still, she suspected that the heat rising in her cheeks gave away just how easily she found herself charmed by the guy. Which was exactly the opposite of what Jo needed today.

She had promised herself to stop playing it safe. She wanted, no, she *needed,* to move forward, to get on with her life. She had so much she hoped to accomplish and so many things she had to deal with before she could even start.

"Weather forecasts notwithstanding, the *Sun Times* is one of the things I came here to talk to you about," she said.

He closed the paper and sat back. "I already have a subscription."

"I'm not *working* for them."

"Oh." Did she detect a hint of disappointment in his tone?

"I am, however, considering working *on* something for them." And by *considering* she meant it was the last thing on earth she wanted to do.

"Oh?" Disappointment shifted quickly to curiosity.

"A letter to the editor on behalf of my family."

"Uh-oh."

Jo winced.

His response had neatly summed up the far-ranging run of emotions she'd felt when Kate had first asked her to take on the chore based on an idea said editor had planted in Moxie's head that Kate had heard of via Vince.

"I know." She plunked into the olive-green faux-leather chair next to the desk and pouted. "I don't want to do it, really."

"Then don't."

She snapped her head up so quickly a puff of her blond bangs fell over her eyebrow and got snagged by her eyelashes. She flicked it away without taking her eyes off the adorable man with the extraordinary suggestions. "Really? You think I could? Or, um, *couldn't?*"

She tried to imagine defying her sister's plea to do this for the good of the Cromwell family. Ignore Kate's wishes? That definitely fell into the "not playing it safe" category.

He leaned toward her, his fingers intertwined atop the loosely folded *Sun Times*. "Are you asking *me* for permission to not do the thing you clearly do not want to do?"

He made it sound like a bad thing.

"Um, no?" she ventured.

He shook his head and gave the faintest chuckle. "Are you even listening to yourself, Jo?"

"Please!" She threw her hands up at last. She had come to him to help her write this letter and here he was trying to talk her out of it. "Enough

83

with the questions already! You really have a thing for questions."

"Just doing my job."

"Giving people headaches?"

"Making people use their heads."

"You see, now, I'd have thought as a minister your specialty would be more in the 'using your heart' department."

"Uh-uh. It's a common fallacy that spirituality manifested in the guise of traditional Christian faith comes from and is synonymous with pure, unempirical, ill-explored emotions, not involving critical thought or requiring intellectual application. It's just not so."

"I got spirituality . . . blah, blah . . . Christian faith . . . blah, blah . . . emotions . . . just not so. The rest? You lost me."

He laughed. "Smart people love God, too."

"Oh!" She nodded and laughed a little, trying not to show her anxiety that her not having gotten what he meant, meant that she wasn't one of the smart people *he* meant. Jo had never felt dumb before but being around Travis rattled her. In a good way, but rattled her nonetheless.

"I just think . . ." He spread his hands as if about to launch into another lengthy diatribe then gave a shrug and through a crooked smile said, "That's all. I *think* and I always want to challenge others to do the same."

"I have enough challenges right now, Travis,

without turning a letter to the editor of the *Sun Times* into one, as well."

"Yeah, but it's not *just* a letter to the editor. It's a letter to the *new* editor of the place you want to call home, written on behalf of your somewhat insulted family. If you don't go into that with your brain fully engaged, you're done for, Jo."

"I *know.* That's why I came to you for your input about it." She put her hand to her forehead and shut her eyes. "Suddenly, I wish I had sprained my wrist instead of my ankle, so I'd have an excuse not to use a pen or a keyboard."

"Yeah. But if you'd sprained your wrist, you'd never have needed my help getting around and then . . ."

She peeked at him from under her hand. "And then what?"

"We wouldn't be where we are today."

Stop playing it safe. If she truly meant that, she couldn't think of a better time to take that first big step than right now. "Where are we today, Travis?"

He gave her a pastor's grin, all wisdom and soothing amusement and not a spark of the mischief that usually passed between them. "Now you're asking hard questions."

It was that grin that made her sit up and speak out. "Hard? I don't think so. It seems pretty straightforward to me."

"Where are we?" he repeated, stretching out each syllable.

She didn't know if that was the mark of a thoughtful minister weighing the situation with utmost care or the age-old tactic of a typical cornered male who didn't want to blow a good thing with a girl but wasn't ready to discuss it head-on.

"To-oo-o-daa-ay."

"Yes!" Stalling. Definitely stalling. He was the one trying to play it safe now. A couple of days ago she would have let him but he was the one who had told her to push herself, to go after her answers, to be smart. "Where are we today, Travis? Are we dating? Are we in a relationship? Are we just—"

He put his hands up to cut her off before she slapped a label on whatever was between them. "You know I have feelings for you, Jo."

She exhaled. "That is such a nonanswer, Travis."

"What do you want to hear?" He pushed away from the desk and stood, looking down at her. "That since the first time I saw you trying to come off cool and classy while hopping around on one foot that I couldn't stop thinking about you?"

"Yes," she said quietly.

At last taking a chance that someone would find her worthy, that someone would love her, and demanding to be seen and acknowledged had paid off.

Travis took a step away. He put his back to her, rubbed his neck then turned and said, over his shoulder, "That when you came down to help me serve breakfast to the hungry and homeless of Santa Sofia I knew there was more to you than anyone, even your own family, suspected and I knew I could fall deeply in love with you?"

"Yes." Quieter still. So quiet she couldn't hear her own voice above the pounding of her heart. The man saw her for herself. Not as the kid no one had any use for. Not as Kate's shadow or as Mike Powers's lackey but as Jo, who had something to offer, as the person she truly wanted to be.

He faced the large window overlooking the beach. "That the minute you began talking about starting a women's ministry here to help others get their lives on track even though you repeatedly refused to get your own house in order—literally and figuratively—that I knew we had no real future together?"

"Ye— No!" Jo felt slapped. Had he really said what she thought he said? "No future?"

He did not look at her. "You asked."

"But I . . . Travis, I . . ."

"There are just way too many questions you can't answer right now, Jo." He turned and placed his hand on the back of his chair. "Or won't."

"Not about you," she protested, still stunned. "I don't have any questions about you, about how I *feel* for you."

"I just explained it to you, Jo. Emotion in and of itself is not a firm enough foundation."

"Love is," she murmured. "Isn't it?"

He did not answer that directly but instead simply told her, "You have a lot of unfinished business, Jo."

"Are you talking about the questions you thought I should be asking myself? I thought those applied to my starting a ministry, not to our starting a relationship."

"I mean the mess you have left behind you in Atlanta."

"Mess? You mean the house?" She had bought the monstrosity when there was money to be made in renovation and quick resale.

Mike Powers, the Realtor she had worked for, had assured her it would be great investment, a fast flip, easy money.

Ambitious and wanting to make a name for herself in the real-estate game, she had sunk every dime she had into the deal. Then borrowed as cost overruns mounted. Now she had a house nobody could afford in an ever-sinking market.

Her whole life she had wanted to step out of her sister Kate's shadow and be noticed. The mess with the house made her want to crawl in a hole and hide.

"The house. The debt." He never took his eyes off her. "Have you done anything about that at all?"

"Does pleading with God for a miracle count?" She held up her hand to stop him from replying to that. "I already know the answer to that."

"Jo, it's not that I'm not attracted to you."

"That's nice to know."

"But as a spiritual leader and, basically, as a guy who knows how much emotional and mental effort it takes to try to change your life as drastically as you say you want to change yours—"

"I do. I do want to change my life, Travis."

"You can't do that by simply selling your expensive shoes."

Jo looked down at the simple sandals on her feet.

"Or by talking a good plan."

"Or by writing a letter," she mumbled. "I know."

"Jo—"

She wanted to be angry with him but how could she be angry with the truth? Especially when it was the conclusion she had come to on her own that day on the beach. Her decision to stop trying to find the safety that had eluded her all her life wasn't about trying to force Travis to make a commitment. It wasn't about finally getting the nerve to stand up to Kate. It was about taking control of her own life. That's what Travis wanted her to do. If she pushed aside her hurt and disappointment and thought about it, she couldn't have asked for a more compassionate demonstration of his real feelings for her than that.

She had to honor that. She had to stand up for herself. Nobody was going to see her for herself until she did that. "I've got to face my problems. Find my answers."

He nodded. "Once you do that, come back and ask me that question again, about where we are, where we're going."

She stood. She wanted to say more but knew if she opened her mouth again, she'd burst into tears. So she managed a weak smile, raised her hand in farewell, turned and headed for the door.

Chapter Eight

Moxie came sailing through the glass front door of the Urgent Care Clinic.

An eerie stillness radiated through the spotless green-and-white reception area amplified by the smell of disinfectant and the soft, incessant buzz and almost imperceptible flicker of the fluorescent lights overhead. The place rarely kept busy, except for late-night weekends and tourist season when things could get downright chaotic. But most of the time, like today, even the intake worker tended to wander off on personal errands, take long lunches or plug herself in to her MP3 player and tune out the world. Moxie didn't know where the rest of the staff was today, only that Dr. Lionel Lloyd had been sitting at the receptionist's desk twirling back and forth in the squeaky blue chair.

"Once burned. Twice shy. Isn't that how the saying goes?" she asked as she stopped directly in front of him.

"You've been burned?" Lionel came rushing around the desk toward her, his disheveled lab coat flapping.

"No. No, not literally burned. Metaphorically." Out of sheer force of habit she met him not with a sweet kiss but with a quick visual once-over.

The man had never learned to make himself presentable and often went off to work looking more like an unambitious mad scientist than a serious medical professional. She reached out to straighten his collar. When she tugged on it from one side, the sleeve on that side jerked up. When she tried to pull the lapels together, the collar bunched up again. She frowned.

"What's wrong?"

You're a grown man. Everyone in town has us on the path to matrimony and yet every time I see you I can't help but think of you more as some kind of fixer-upper than as my home sweet home. That's what's wrong. Moxie twisted her mouth to one side and looked him over again and said merely, "I'm not sure."

He slid his glasses off and cleaned the lenses with his hastily tied tie as he asked, "You've been metaphorically burned but you're not sure what's wrong?"

"Hmm?" She looked him in the eye at last. She'd been in the clinic for five minutes and this was the first time she'd looked into the eyes of the man she supposedly loved. And all she could think was . . .

When she had looked into Lionel's eyes, her

mind had instantly flashed to yesterday's encounter with R. Hunt Diamante.

She stiffened. "Nothing's wrong."

"But you said—"

"I'm just mad at my sister, that's all." That wasn't all.

"Your *sister.* I still can't get used to you saying that."

"Welcome to the club." She rubbed her temple, but that didn't ease the tension tightening like a band around her head. She wanted to lay the blame for her discomfort on her sisters and newly found mother, but in truth they were just one more brick in the wall Moxie felt rising up around her, closing her in.

Jo, Kate, Dodie, the infamous and fatherly Billy J, even Lionel, all added to the sense that she was quickly losing the independence she had asserted over her own life as a teenager. "Ever since my foster mom left Dad and me, I always felt a certain amount of pride in knowing I could take care of myself."

He slid his glasses back on and peered at her. "Dad?"

She didn't know if her remark confused or intrigued him.

Intrigued, she decided, though the way the man couldn't seem to even manage to roll the sleeves up on his labcoat presented a strong case for con-fused. He had a point, either way, because up until recently she usually referred to her foster father as Billy J when talking about him to other people, especially around Santa Sofia where that's how absolutely everybody knew him. But now it seemed more important to identify him in the way she felt about it. Now that her whole story had unfolded about her birth father having taken her and eventually given her away and with the arrival of . . .

"And now I have *these people,*" she went on as she attacked his uneven sleeve situation.

"Your sisters."

"Yes. I have these *sisters.*" She unrolled the right sleeve of his wonky lab coat and began turning it up, trying to keep the fabric from bunching. "*And* a mother that I never even knew about. But they knew about me, you see?"

"I suppose so."

As she spoke her emotions got the better of her and with every word she uttered the sleeve got higher and more crumpled. "And so they have all these expectations, they want me to step into this . . . this . . ."

"Role?"

Moxie had been thinking *trap* or perhaps *strait-jacket.* But for this discussion's purposes . . .

"Okay, role. The role of Molly Christina, baby sister. The little lost lamb who's been found again and should be grateful to be back in the fold again." She moved the left sleeve and tackled it with the same fervor as the right one, propelled by her escalating emotions. "Except I don't want to be in the fold. I want to be free."

"Moxie!" He shook his arm to free himself of her nearly manic coat-sleeve-rolling. In seconds he had shaken the fabric loose and began trying to no avail to smooth it out as he said, "What does all that have to do with being burned?"

"Jo asked me to write something for the paper in response to the article about 'our' family." She made quote marks in the air.

He looked at her blankly.

"I wouldn't mind that, of course, but yesterday the whole family—" more quote marks with crooked fingers "—had to get together to read the original article together."

"All of you?"

"All of us reading one lone newspaper at the same time in Dodie, Jo and Kate's kitchen. A bit too much togetherness in that, if you ask me. Like we couldn't all just read it on our own then maybe make some phone calls to talk it over?"

"Hardly seems like enough to get this worked up over."

"It wouldn't be, I suppose, except Jo asked me to come to the beach to help her start a group there."

"What's that got to do with the newspaper

article and her asking you to write something else?"

"My point exactly." She stabbed her finger at him.

"She didn't *start* anything."

Moxie replayed the frustrating encounter in her head leading her inevitably to another encounter she had had shortly after that. *R. Hunt Diamante.* She clenched her jaw. "On second thought, maybe she did."

"Did what?"

"Start something." She gave the man a "please try to keep up" pat on the arm and dived head-long back into voicing her theory. "Because in the end she excused all of her wishy-washiness about starting a group, not starting a group, whatever, by making this big, emphatic announcement saying that she wasn't going to play it safe."

"Play *what* safe?"

"I don't know, really." She only knew how her sister's emphasis on the idea had affected her and how that eventually led to her embarrassing herself in front of the new newspaper editor.

That's what she was really mad about. Not about her sister's total disregard for her time, but for the way Jo or Kate or Dodie could get her worked up into such an emotional state that she made a fool of herself.

"I'm still lost, Moxie. Where does the twice shy part come in?"

She bit her lower lip to keep herself from furthering her humiliation by repeating the tale of the overwrought maiden in distress mistaking the town's newest citizen for Road Rage Pharaoh.

"I'm just saying I'm stressing a little here, Lionel, and I wanted a little . . ." She turned to smile at him, squinted, then sighed. "Lionel, you have on Kate's lab coat."

"Do I?" He looked at the name tag and laughed. "I'm not used to having another one hanging on my hook. The residents usually bring their own."

"Are you two still sharing an office?"

"For now." He slid off Kate's lab coat then hung it on a row of hooks attached to the back of the intake office door. "What with her only here part-time."

"Only here when she feels like it," Moxie corrected. While she had found much to admire and even love about her oldest sister, Moxie couldn't help noticing a pattern among the Cromwell sisters. "Don't let her boss you around. She has a dominant personality and doesn't hesitate to tell people what she wants from them."

"Are you giving me advice or talking about your own, shall we say, *burning* issues?" He gave her a wry yet knowing smile.

"Got me," she confessed. "But still . . ."

He shrugged into his own coat.

She stepped forward and looped his stethoscope around his neck, straightened his name tag and stepped back to admire her handiwork. "I just want you to look out for yourself."

"Isn't that what I have you for, Moxie?"

She studied the title, Lionel Lloyd, M.D., and sighed. "Doesn't really seem like enough, does it?"

"What doesn't?"

"Me looking out for you." She finally said what had been on her mind for quite some time now. "It doesn't really seem like enough to build a marriage on."

"Doesn't it?" Everything from his tone to the distant look in his eyes suggested he was asking himself this and not her.

"I think you know the answer to that, Li." Speaking softly, she prodded him to consider it all a moment.

He did. Casting his gaze away, he stared out the window for several long moments before finally looking her in the eyes again. He exhaled, making his shoulders slope forward, and tilted his head to one side. "Moxie, are you breaking up with me?"

"I think I am." Shouldn't she feel sadder about that? Or sad at all?

Moxie took only a few seconds to marvel at that and to try to distinguish just what emotions she was feeling. When she couldn't instantly pinpoint them, she figured they could wait and she turned her attention to Lionel. "I didn't come here with that in mind. It just sort of came around to that conclusion."

He nodded. "It's *been* coming around to that conclusion for a while now. Neither of us just said it out loud."

"I guess the stress and pressure of dealing with my new situation has sort of made me feel the need to . . ." How could she put this considerately?

"Create a little more space in your life?"

Not very considerate but a good way of putting it. "You don't seem all that upset by this," she noted.

"Hey, just because I'm easily distracted doesn't mean I'm easily fooled." He tugged at the lapels of his coat. "I've pushed for us to make our engagement official for a long time now and you've kept putting me off. I knew the chances of us making the big leap were pretty slim."

She nodded awkwardly, trying to think what they might have left unsaid, trying to come up with a gracious way to say goodbye and get out.

Finally, Lionel cleared his throat, folded his hands together behind his back and asked, "So. How long do you think we should, uh, um, mourn?"

"Mourn?" It didn't seem like the right term.

"We did date for a long time," he justified.

"Hmm. True." She almost blurted out, "But my heart wasn't really in it for a while now," but caught herself. If she said that much, she might say *too* much. Not that she had anything to hide, no potential new love waiting in the wings. "Hey!" She jerked her head up. "Why do you want to know about the proper 'mourning' period for our relationship? That's the kind of thing people say when they are trying to decide how long to wait before they jump into a new relationship."

"Just, um . . ."

"There's somebody you want to ask out, isn't there?"

"I didn't, honest, Moxie. But since you broke up with me, well, I can think of someone."

"Someone I know?" She had no right to be so nosy. Or so bossy, making that kind of demand. She supposed if he confronted her about that, she could rightly call it a Cromwell family trait.

"I don't think you know her. You might. Possibly you do."

"Possibly?" That meant *probably.* She told herself it was her pride more than her feelings that were hurt by this news. "I guess the only way to know for sure is for you to tell me who she is."

"Just one of the new residents taking shifts here at the clinic recently."

"A resident? That works here?" Moxie could hardly believe her ears.

"Nothing's happened, Moxie. I don't even know if she would consider going out with me."

"And if she does, then what? You two get involved and decide you don't need Kate around here anymore and squeeze her out completely?"

"What? I don't have any plans to . . . And didn't you just tell me a few minutes ago not to let Kate boss me around? Now you think I'm going to go behind her back and—how'd you put it?— squeeze her out?" He laughed. "Where your sister is concerned, Mox, you don't even seem to know your own mind."

"Oh, I know my mind." It wasn't a lie. She did know her mind. It was her conflicting emotions toward her family that had her tangled in knots. She met his bewildered gaze with cool determination. "Whatever happens between you and this resident, promise me that you will deal squarely with Kate."

"You know I will."

"I want to believe that, Lionel. You've never given me any reason to think otherwise. But—" Moxie looked at Kate's lab coat hanging on the hook "—while I might complain about Kate and want to tell her to go eat a bug because sometimes she gets on my very last nerve, I will totally kick the behind of anyone who does anything to hurt her. Got it?"

"Yeah, I got it, Mox." He laughed, deep and genuine and clearly a little bit at her expense. "Despite your every effort to avoid it, you're beginning to be a real—"

"Watch it," she warned.

"Sister," he concluded.

"Sister," she whispered. Huh. She blinked a few times then cocked her head. "Ya think?"

"Yeah," he muttered before coming to her and hugging her. "Take care of yourself, Moxie. It's been fun. You'll always have a special place in my heart and in my prayers."

She looked up at him and mouthed a thank-you.

The briefest of kisses followed then Moxie turned and moments later stepped out into the bright November morning feeling lighter somehow.

Letting go of Lionel, walking away from that relationship which clearly hadn't served either of them for some time, emboldened her. So did the notion that she could stand up to her family and still be . . .

"A sister," she murmured, somewhat awestruck.

She could do this. She could make more room in her life. More room for her dreams. Her work. Her life.

She'd start by steadfastly refusing to help Jo write that ridiculous letter to the editor.

The editor.

Just the thought of the man's title made her want to . . .

Well, do anything but what *he'd* suggested she do, write an article. Wasn't that basically *his* job?

Wait. He had told *her* to do that. Why had Jo suddenly horned in and taken over?

Not that Moxie wanted to write anything but R. Hunt Diamante had invited her to do it. Not Jo.

Once burned. Twice shy.

Wrong.

Moxie was anything but shy. She was going to tell her new family just that.

Breaking up with Lionel had created some much-needed space in her life. It also inspired her to make a little more. To ask these people who were closing in on her to back off. Although they were very important to her, they were making her feel . . .

"Moxie, I am so glad you're here!" Dodie hopped out of her car, flushed and frantic, which Moxie had come to suspect was the woman's natural state.

"Dodie, you didn't have to track me down. You could have just—" Her hand froze halfway to her cell phone as the older woman rushed to the passenger door, popped it open and a parrot feather stuck in a hat fell out.

"Come and help me with Billy J. I think he's having a heart attack."

Chapter Nine

Kate shut her eyes and sank back against the arm of the couch, not sure of her next move.

Her mother was terrified.

Billy J could well be experiencing a life-threatening episode.

Jo was who knew where.

Kate was stuck at the cottage.

She'd never felt so helpless in her life. At that moment her thoughts touched back on the evening before and the look on Vince's face when Gentry broke the news of his impending move. Kate had felt plenty helpless then, too.

She had wanted to show support for Gentry and tell him how happy she was for his new opportunity. But she didn't have to see the worried expression on Vince's face or suffer the virtual black cloud of his grim mood that settled over the rest of the evening to know he would have seen that as a betrayal. Or an intrusion.

Either way it would have forced a wedge between them that their relationship might not have recovered from. So Kate had reminded them all that her foot ached—not a lie, her foot *always* ached—and asked Vince to take her home early.

She'd gone to her room, not wanting to rehash the details with Jo or their mother, and tried not to think about any of it, about any of them. When she couldn't sleep, she'd taken some medication prescribed by her own physician—something she didn't do often—and conked out, oblivious to the comings and goings around her. She had awoken a little disoriented, dressed, then gone downstairs to see if a cup of strong coffee could chase away the last of her gloomy mood and grogginess from her medicine. Until Dodie had called on her way to the clinic moments ago, Kate had assumed both her mom and sister were still at home.

She sighed, then turned to make her way back to the kitchen and the phone so she could call the clinic and see if anyone could come get her or at least update her on the Billy J situation. Helpless did not begin to cover her feelings about that. First she hadn't had enough metaphorical backbone to stand up and speak her mind to Vince about the kids and now she couldn't come to Billy J's aid because she literally did not have strong enough footbones to get herself to the clinic under her own power.

Her head hurt and the light from the window didn't help. She had just put her hand up to cover her eyes when the sound of a car engine made her jerk her head up. "Vince!"

The kids must have left Fabbie with Vince overnight, and he was bringing her home to them now.

She winced at the light but that quickly shifted into squinty-eyed determination. She lunged, flailed, almost fell, then lunged again and in two attempts had propelled herself to the front door. She swung it open, swallowed to keep the nausea and dull pain down and bellowed, "Vince! You have to take me to the Urgent Care Clinic right now. Mom is on her way there with Billy J—it's an emergency!"

Like a well-practiced troop of circus performers, everyone fell into step.

Gentry ran to get Kate's cane.

Pera got the baby out of her car seat, gathered up the baby's things, then held the door open for Kate to climb in.

Vince took the cane from Gentry, stashed it behind the seat then slid behind the wheel.

"Will Billy J be all right?" Gentry asked as he helped Kate into her seat.

"I don't know. Could be his heart." Kate clicked her seat belt.

"His heart?" Gentry squinted. "Aren't you a foot doctor?"

"And an E.R. specialist," Vince reminded him.

"More importantly, I'm family." Kate took a deep breath, unsure how Vince, or Gentry for that matter, would respond when she added, "When your family needs you, even if it's not your blood relative, you drop everything and are there for them."

"That's my cue," Vince told his son. He slammed the driver's-side door, gave his son a "catch you later" wave and gunned the motor of his pickup truck.

"Thank you so much for doing this," she said as they took off along the side roads of Santa Sofia.

"That's what families do." He smiled.

Her stomach fluttered. "Is that how you feel? That we're family?"

"I guess the true test of that is whether you're willing to do for me what you're doing for your mom, Moxie and Billy J." He did not throw it out there like a challenge but matter-of-factly. This is how things are. "If it comes down to it, Kate, and I need you to, do you think you might drop everything and be there for me?"

Propose.

She fixed her eyes on his and willed it. *Just ask me.* She couldn't very well say yes to the vagaries of "if it comes down to it," "do you think" or "would you drop everything." *Say the words. Ask me to marry you.*

She shifted in her seat. She could not take her eyes off him. Her skin tingled with the anticipation more of what he left unsaid, the possibilities. The air in the truck cab practically crackled.

Propose now, please.

"Will you . . ."

Marry me.

"Need me to go on after I drop you off?"

"Yes!"

"All right then."

Kate winced. "I just meant that . . ."

"No, I understand. You've got to focus on Billy J. On gathering your resources for helping him."

She should. The healer in her felt a twinge of guilt that she'd let her focus shift to personal issues.

After Vince pulled into a staff parking space, he quickly retrieved her cane, handed it to her and got out of his truck.

He looked so strong, so sure of himself, so capable and yet so vulnerable.

She gripped the brass cat's head topper of her cane and swung her legs gingerly out the truck door. He stuck out his arm to lend her support as she climbed out. She pushed her door open and he finished pulling it open.

"I won't stay. But if you don't mind, I'd like to go in and find out what's going on with Billy J, and if I can do anything for Moxie."

She started to tell him it wasn't necessary, that she'd call him when she knew more. But before she could find the words to say it without snapping and maybe showing just a hint of her disappointment that he had just blurted out his feelings, Jo and Travis came rolling into the parking lot in her bright blue PT Cruiser.

"It's going to get awfully crowded in the clinic if this keeps up!" She met Vince's gaze.

He smiled a little at her and took her hand to help her steady her injured foot on the ground. "That's what family does. When there's a need, they go. They don't let anything stand between them and their loved ones."

She nodded and, even as Travis and Jo got out of her car and started up the walk, took a long stride toward the clinic. She really didn't think she needed to hang around for the extended version of a lecture on the lengths to which families go for one another. Especially when she wasn't sure who Vince counted as her family and just how far he wanted her to go.

"Don't y'all take another step!" Dodie came rushing out at them, her hands extended, her eyes wide, her usually perfectly coiffed hair windblown and about as stylish as a wrecked bird's nest.

"What's going on?" Jo asked.

She, Travis, Vince and Kate all completely ignored Dodie's decree and rushed forward. Apparently all of them adhered to that "not letting anything stand in your way" creed.

"I think only Kate should go inside." Dodie stepped forward, tugged her oldest daughter by the arm and then gave her the gentlest of shoves toward the door. "Given the circumstances, she's the only one of us I think necessary, the only one that would be welcome."

Kate couldn't help it—she felt a twinge of pride in being singled out. She didn't know where she stood precisely with Vince but clearly she was needed here.

Kate took another elongated stride, then reached for the door with her free hand, her head up in readiness to meet the situation both as a medical doctor for Billy J and as the designated comfort-giver to her youngest sister. She pulled the door open.

"I wouldn't go back in there for all the tea in China," Dodie said.

As a blast of cold air whooshed into Kate's face, she heard her mother tell the group why.

"Right now, Molly Christina is so mad she could spit fire and I think if she *could* spit fire, she'd spit that fire at *all* of us."

Chapter Ten

"Please, Daddy, please, hang in there. Don't . . ." Moxie couldn't bring herself to actually voice her greatest fears out loud.

Silently, though, deep in the places where she didn't have to hide anything, she offered her most profound prayers to her heavenly Father. *Don't let my daddy die. Not now. Not when things are so uncertain. Not when I still need him so much.*

She gave Billy J's large, leathery hand a squeeze. Her throat had gone so dry it hurt. She could not seem to swallow. She blinked. Tears bathed the view of Lionel hovering over her father, applying sensors hooked to a heart monitor.

The nurse on duty moved quickly.

Moxie stroked her father's thin white hair to get it off his ruddy, round face. "Just *don't,* okay?"

Billy J started to speak but only managed to croak out her name before convulsing in a raspy, rattling coughing fit.

"Should I get some water?" Moxie twisted one way then turned the other, not sure what to do.

The nurse pushed past her and began to draw blood.

Moxie's knees went weak. She pressed the back of her hand to her mouth.

Lionel moved to the monitor then threw a glance at her over his shoulder. "Why don't you go check on your . . ."

Moxie rallied enough to glower at him, her only warning against him invoking "that word."

"Why don't you check on Dodie?" he tried again, wisely circumventing the touchy topic of family. "You were awfully hard on her."

"Can you blame me?" Moxie clung to Billy J's hand. "My father, the only father I've ever known, is having a heart attack and as she rushes him to the E.R., she calls everyone she knows in town but me?"

"First off . . ." Lionel took her by the shoulders firmly, much more firmly than he ever had while they were dating. Very confident. Very *doctorly.*

Moxie had never seen this aspect of him. Well, not from this side of things, not as a patient or the patient's next of kin . . . next of kin. That's who they notified when the worst happened. "My father is having a heart attack, Li. Shouldn't you be doing something?"

"First off," he began again. "Your father is not having a heart attack."

Moxie exhaled in a whoosh, dispensing some of the gathering tension in her body. "What about the pain in his chest, the trouble breathing, his inability to focus?"

"We'll need more tests but all signs point to the pain and the breathing as lung-related."

Billy J let loose with another barrage of racking coughs. When he finished, he heaved a weary sigh then asked the nurse if this was a "nonsmoking" emergency room.

"The inability to focus?" Lionel leaned in to make himself heard above Billy J's fit. "Well, are you really sure that's a new thing?"

The hair on the back of Moxie's neck bristled. "My father is possibly dying and you're making jokes?"

Lionel held her arms tighter. "Your father is not dying. There's definitely a problem, but he's not at risk from immediate death."

She relaxed a little more. She wanted to believe him. "Are you sure?"

"I went to one of the best medical schools in the country, Mox. Trust that I learned a thing or two there."

"About potential heart attacks?"

"No, about never telling a patient you know *for sure* about anything!"

"Lionel!"

His grasp on her transformed into a hug. "I wouldn't joke if I didn't think your dad was going to be all right."

"Really?"

"Really." He gave her a kiss on the forehead.

That's when Moxie realized he had quietly, compassionately and adamantly moved her from her father's bedside to the door.

"Do you have any idea what's wrong with him?"

"I'm thinking pneumonia." He opened the door.

"Pneumonia?" In one way she felt relieved. "That's better than a heart attack, isn't it? It's treatable, right?"

"It's treatable, but still very serious, given his age and the generally poor state of his overall health." He prodded her to go on into the hallway.

She held her ground as tension began to coil again through her body. "Will he be all right?"

A frown flicked over his face. He adjusted his glasses. "Pneumonia is tricky."

That didn't answer her question. Or did it?

"I think, to be safe, after I check him out, maybe see if I can give him something to make him more comfortable, you ought to take him straight over to the hospital. I'll call over to let them know he's on his way and leave it up to the docs there to decide if they want to keep him or send him home with meds."

Moxie tried to take it all in, tried to figure out what she needed to do for every eventuality. Take her father, get meds, bring him home, take time off work to take care of him.

"Why don't you go make whatever arrange-

114

ments you need to and let me get back to your dad?"

Now she was the one having shortness of breath. First things first, she decided. Otherwise it would all overwhelm her. "Okay. Let's see, the hospital is over forty minutes away. You think he'll be all right for the ride?"

"Do you want me to order an ambulance?"

"Does he *need* an ambulance?"

"No." Another insistent push and he had her outside the room. "Just thought it might be the easiest way to transport him. You can't exactly use your truck."

"What's wrong with my truck?" She held her hand up. "Don't answer."

"Moxie, I have a patient to tend to. The sooner I take care of him the sooner you can be on your way and then—"

"Then what, Li? I don't know how I can handle this alone."

"You're not alone, Moxie."

"That's true." She clenched her teeth. "I'm *never* alone."

"That's the way to talk." He gave her arm a pat.

"I didn't mean it was a good thing. I meant that since the Cromwell family came back to Santa Sofia they are always—"

"I'm here!" Kate came practically careening around the corner. Her cane swinging in one hand, she used her outstretched arm to counterbalance. This kept her rocking gait rolling until she reached them. "Lionel? Where's Billy J? What do you need me to do?"

"Everything is under control." Moxie looked to Lionel for confirmation.

He gave her a nod and disappeared into the room to see about Billy J.

Moxie drew a deep breath and pressed on. "So why don't you deal with Dodie? You can take her home, I'll stay with my dad and I'll call you later when we know more about what's going on."

"What's going on, y'all?" Vince rounded the corner then pulled up short when Moxie turned to face him.

She must have looked a sight as he not only stopped in his tracks and in mid-sentence, but also threw his hands up to keep the people following close on his heels from coming any closer to her.

Jo all but smashed her pretty little nose into the man's broad back.

Travis had to make a quick side step to keep from plowing into Jo.

However, Dodie, wringing a tattered tissue in her plump little hands, bypassed them all. "I couldn't convince any of them to stay outside. The whole family insisted on coming in."

"Family." That word again! *Family?* A couple months ago they were all strangers to me, *and* to my dad."

"Molly, sweetheart, we only want to help." Dodie sounded apologetic and yet firm in her conviction.

"I understand that, but do you always have to help from so close?" She laced her arms tightly over her chest and pulled her shoulders up. This kept her from actually swinging her elbows out to physically create more room and gave her just enough comfort to keep from bursting out crying. Moxie tried to keep her anger and frustration low-key but it wasn't easy. Her father's health scare had really gotten to her and the fact that she only learned about it by accident didn't ease her mind any. "It's just so . . . overwhelming."

Travis stepped forward. "Look, I know you're under a lot of stress right now, Moxie, but Dodie and the girls only thought—"

"Of themselves." She filled in the blank with quiet conviction.

"What?"

"Dodie and the girls only thought of themselves." She spoke softly, saying what she thought had to finally be said. She did not lash out. She did not allow her voice to quiver. She took a deep breath and talked from her hurting heart to the people who claimed to want only the best for her. "You said when there is trouble, family goes—well, doesn't family also *include* each other? Don't they take the other members of that family into account?"

"Molly Christina, that's no way to talk to us when we only wanted to—"

"My name is Moxie." She almost stamped her foot, just like a petulant child. "And don't try to pull that maternal guilt card on me, Dodie."

Everyone seemed to take a quick gasping breath at that.

Moxie didn't care. Well, she *cared,* she just didn't see any other way to get her point across except to stop caring about how these people would feel and let them know how *she* felt.

"It was one thing when you simply crowded into my life." She thought of all the examples she could give but decided that was not the point; the point was . . . "Today you tried to crowd me *out* of my dad's life or, worse, a threat to his life."

"I am so sorry." Dodie reached out to touch Moxie's cheek.

Moxie flinched, just enough that the woman's finger only grazed her hair instead of brushing her face.

"You thought my dad's life might be in danger and you called everyone . . ." Moxie pressed her lips together but they still trembled with the emotion she wanted so desperately to hold back. "Everyone *but* me."

"It was a gut reaction, honey." Dodie stroked her arm. "It made sense at the time. I called Kate because she's a doctor and then Jo because I knew she could find Travis and get him here."

"Not because it mattered whether *I* knew or not," Jo mumbled in a way that seemed half humorous and appeasement for Moxie's sake, half hurt little kid straight from her own heart.

"I was making calls fast and furious as I tried to get Billy J here," Dodie went on. She sounded truly sorry about the oversight but not upset about Moxie's rudeness brought on by her injured feelings.

"I had to drive Kate," Vince volunteered. "But you can bet your bait bucket that if I knew you and Billy J needed help, nothing could keep me away."

"Thanks." Moxie smiled at the man she considered a big brother to her.

"I came because I thought Lionel could use backup," Kate snapped. "So I'm going in there to see what I can do to help."

"No help necessary." Lionel came through the door again with a file in his hand. "Though, if you'd like, you can go in, look him over and see if you concur with my diagnosis."

"Diagnosis?" Dodie stepped forward.

Everyone else pressed in behind her.

"What is it?"

"Is he okay?"

"What can we do to help?"

Moxie held her arms close in at her sides and shifted her feet to keep anyone from trampling her toes. It was as though they hadn't heard her

119

diatribe about backing off at all.

"It's not a heart attack," Lionel assured the group.

"Thank the Lord," Dodie whispered, her hand over her heart.

Vince exhaled and stepped away to rest his back against the wall. "That's great news."

"Jo and I prayed the whole way over here." Travis took Moxie's hand and gave it a squeeze.

Suddenly Moxie felt just awful. They had come and crowded in and ignored her ugly reaction because they cared about her father and about her and she had acted so . . . "I wasn't really angry at you, just . . ."

"Scared." Dodie did caress Moxie's cheek this time. "I know. And hurt."

"Yeah."

"And you had every right to feel that way." Dodie's gaze searched Moxie's face.

Tears shimmered in the woman's eyes. Eyes that seemed to Moxie like those of a stranger and at the same time so familiar that she felt she had looked into them a thousand times and every one of those times found love and acceptance.

"You should have been my very first call, Moll . . . um . . . Moxie, sweetheart."

"Thanks."

"I'll stop and take your feelings into account before I do anything like that again." Dodie gave Moxie a hug.

For the first time since she'd begun feeling hemmed in by this new situation, Moxie returned the gesture. Tentatively but without reservation. "That means a lot to me."

Moxie let go and started to step away.

Dodie kept holding her.

Mom. The woman clearly wanted Moxie to say, "That means a lot to me, *Mom.*"

Moxie wanted to comply but then stopped herself. Calling Dodie *Mom* was not something she could do lightly. It was, in essence, acknowledging a bond had formed between them. One of the greatest bonds in all human nature. Mother and daughter. Was Moxie ready for that?

She didn't know. That was answer enough to keep her from blurting it out just to free herself from the awkwardness of the moment.

She had promised herself she would set boundaries. She had begun that work by letting Dodie know how much her thoughtless exclusion of Moxie had hurt. The Cromwells respected her in a totally new way now. No more running roughshod over her emotions based on their own notions of family and the proper pecking order.

That made Moxie smile, her conviction that Kate and Jo and Dodie would back off a little now. They would give her room to breathe. Allow her to take her time to sort out what she wanted and how she wanted to approach things.

"Okay. Kate concurs with my diagnosis of

pneumonia." Lionel stepped into the hallway, clapping his hands together. "I'm sending him to be checked out at the hospital. Have you decided how you want to get him there?"

Moxie opened her mouth.

"I'll take him," Dodie volunteered. "I have the most comfortable car. Y'all can come along, too. Plenty of room."

No, there's not! Moxie held her breath to keep from shouting it right there in the hallway. There was not enough room in the whole state of Florida if this was how Dodie planned to do things—to promise to back off and defer to Moxie one minute then the first time a decision must be made she up and says—

"Hello? I'm here." A strong, masculine voice with a Northern accent rang out from the lobby. "Have an appointment to talk to the doctor about doing some advertising with the *Sun Times?*"

"Great!" Moxie recognized the voice and the accent immediately. Just what she needed to put the cherry on the top of this rancid ice-cream sundae of a day.

"I'll tell him you need to reschedule," Vince said to Lionel.

"We'll all go." Dodie turned to lead the way. "Then we can hop in our cars and caravan to the hospital."

The whole group turned and hurried down the hallway.

Moxie looked at Lionel. "They're doing it again."

"Doing what?"

"Crowding me out of my own dad's life."

"They are just trying to be helpful." Lionel gave her a smirk then shook his head. "You have to get your dad to the hospital and you can't use your truck. Who else are you going to rely on if not your family?"

Moxie shut her eyes. She could just imagine her old truck stalled in the road, needing help, having to rely on who knew what kind of character to . . .

"Leave that to me, Lionel. I have a great idea." She hurried to cut the group off before they reached the lobby. Boundary setting in the most primitive but effective way. "Well, not a *great* idea, but it's going to have to do."

Chapter Eleven

"The Bait Shack does not need to run no full-page ad in the *Sun Times* to draw in customers."

"Shh, Daddy." Moxie gave the heavyset sixty-something man a push toward the white Mustang convertible in the parking lot. "Think of it as a goodwill gesture to thank our patrons and show support for our local paper."

"Graft is what you mean. You offered that new editor an ad in exchange for the favor."

"That's not exactly how I look at it." Moxie meant that. The truth was she had always thought her father had skimped on marketing and failed to spread his success among other local businesses. "Now, do you want to sit in the front or backseat?"

Billy J jerked his arm away from Moxie's guiding hand, yanked open the door and lumbered into the backseat.

"Now I see how I came by my 'does not play well with others' attitude toward family members," she muttered.

"No." Billy J held his hand up to stop her cold as she tried to climb in behind him. "I'm fine. I don't need you to ride alongside me and hold my hand like I was some tantrum-throwing kid."

Moxie chuckled to herself, then leaned in and planted a big smacking kiss on his warm, ruddy cheek. "If I stop treating you like a tantrum-prone kid, you might stop acting like a kid, Daddy. Where would be the fun in life for me in that?"

He turned his head and smiled sweetly, his voice husky from both his sickness and sentiment as he said, "We have had a lot of fun together, haven't we, girl?"

"We sure have, Dad."

"And nothing in the world is going to change that, right?" he asked.

"Change?" Just that quickly, Moxie realized she wasn't the only one feeling more than a little displaced by the recent Cromwell invasion. "No, Daddy, nothing in the world will ever change how I feel about you."

"How we feel about each other," he corrected.

She kissed his cheek again, then made sure he was buckled in before she closed the back door. She gave a wave to the cluster of people each trying to get an eyeful of her exit from behind the glass door of the clinic.

Moxie practically hopped into the front passenger seat, only to find the *Santa Sofia Sun Times*'s new editor behind the steering wheel, staring at her.

"What?" she asked as she ran her curved fingers through her thick, blond hair.

"Nothing." R. Hunt Diamante shook his head. His dark eyes—strike that, she gave herself a mental directive—his *warm brown* eyes glinted in ill-disguised delight. Charmed, no doubt, by the endearing father-daughter interaction. Or was it something more?

He probably regretted the shoddy way he'd written about her, about all of them in his haphazard article.

Moxie was a great believer in confession being good for the soul. Far be it from her then to deny the poor guy a shot at clearing his conscience and grabbing the small but satisfying slice of inner peace that would come with it.

"Aw, c'mon. It's not nothing," she prodded. "I can tell, you've got something on your mind. You don't have to be afraid to share it with me."

"Afraid?" The warmth in his eyes cooled considerably.

Moxie had obviously hit a nerve.

He reached for the key and started to turn it in the ignition. "Only thing I'm afraid of, sister—"

"I am not your sister." She had hit a nerve in him and he had hit one right back in her. "I'm not sure I want to be *anybody's* sister, buddy."

She glanced up. Her entire family stood with their noses practically pressed against the glass door like puppies in a pet-store window.

"I just wanted to make the point that—"

"Can you make your point and drive at the same time?" She slumped down in her seat and motioned toward the road. "In case you've forgotten, my father is very ill and you agreed to take him to the hospital."

"Agreed?" Billy J practically yelped the word, then fell into a short bout of shallow coughing before he managed to rage on. "That's a pile of big, fat—"

"Daddy."

"Parrot feathers," he concluded. "You bargained for this service at the exorbitant rate of a full-page ad in his struggling weekly paper. I just hope he runs that paper better than he honors his commitment to drive me to the hospital."

"Is that what you're waiting for?" She motioned to the road again. "You want payment in full up front before you'll budge an inch?"

"I wouldn't be moved a fraction of a sliver of a centimeter for all the money in the world."

"Is that right?"

"That's right. I'm doing this because it's the right thing to do." He backed up that claim by pulling out of the parking spot at last, handling the steering wheel with deftness and power. When he stopped to shift gears, Hunt narrowed his eyes on her. "Which, by the way, was the same reason I got out of my car to see if you needed help when I found you seemingly stranded at that stop sign the other day."

127

She drew a breath, ready to give as good as she got. "What are you talking about?"

"That day, I got out to help you and you drove off, then when we crossed paths later, you treated me like some kind of . . ." He searched for the right word.

"Road Rage Pharaoh?" she suggested timidly.

"What?"

She touched her finger to her chin on the spot that correlated to the place on his face where he sported facial hair. "The second I saw you I thought you looked like the picture of Pharaoh from Sunday school."

"Yeah?" Hunt smiled slightly at that.

She nodded.

His smile started to broaden, then froze. "Was Pharaoh a good guy or a bad guy?"

"Wel-l-l-l . . ." For a second she felt torn between giving him a quick Bible lesson and asking him outright why he didn't know. The truth was, she wanted him to know. His little speech about taking them to the hospital because it was the right thing to do was all good and well but if he wasn't a man of faith, she couldn't imagine how he would fit into her world.

"What are you two going on about?" Billy J slapped his hand on the back of the seat. "Pharaoh? Don't you know your Bible, boy?"

"I, um, I haven't been in a Bible study in a few years." He gave one of those looks that said he knew he should know more about the Bible and get to church more often. "I just wanted a little clarification."

"Only clarification you need is clarifying to me and my daughter whether or not you are ever going to get this car heading to the hospital."

"I am," Hunt assured him, gunning the motor. "And if you don't really want that ad—"

"We don't!" Billy J sputtered through another round of coughing.

"The ad stays." Moxie said it as much for her dad as she did for Hunt.

"It won't make a bit of difference." Hunt looked only at her. "I'll still drive you."

"I know," she said quietly.

He took off. When she had first asked him to take them, he had assured her he knew exactly where they were going. He proved it now by heading for the highway leading west out of Santa Sofia.

Moxie eased her shoulders back against the black leather seat. The very act of leaving Santa Sofia, even under these shaky circumstances, seemed to lift a weight off her shoulders.

The sleepy town, once a tourist haven, had been the only home she had known. It held all her happiest memories, and her most painful ones. Now it seemed only to hold problems. And her new family.

They were one and the same.

She put her head in her hands. "Why does everything always come back to them?"

"Excuse me?" Hunt glanced her way.

She shook her head. The man did not care enough about her family to get the details of their story right. He certainly didn't want to spend the whole time he was doing her a favor hearing her go on and on about them.

In fact, he'd heard quite enough out of her. She thought of their confrontation at the Bait Shack. Heat rose in her cheeks. It didn't matter whether the ancient pharaohs were good or bad, this guy was definitely the good variety. She sighed, laid her head back then rolled it to the side to look at him. "Thanks."

"S'all right. I know you're worried about your dad. I'll get you to the hospital, no problem."

"Thanks for that, too."

"Too?"

"The first thanks was for stopping to help me in my truck."

"Thanks for . . . the thanks." He laughed.

She liked it when he laughed. "And I promise, we will take out that full-page ad. Right, Daddy?"

Z-zno-o-o-orp.

A great, shuddering snore came from the back-seat.

"He fell asleep." She looked at the man behind the wheel.

"He's sick."

"He must be awfully sick." Once Lionel had released her dad and the old guy had acted his normal ornery self, she had put out of her mind how delicate her father's condition might be. "He didn't even hang in the argument long enough to give up and tell me the Weatherby family motto."

"Motto?"

She swallowed hard to try to keep her tears at bay. "When the going gets tough, the Weatherbys go fishing."

He smiled. "I think I like your dad."

"Then do me a favor and get him to the hospital as fast as you can."

Chapter Twelve

"Where ya going?" Travis got out of his car and headed up the drive of the cottage on Dream Away Bay Court.

"I thought we weren't going to ask that question again until I faced my past and dealt with my old problems." Jo did not break stride. She moved away from the house, one foot in front of the other, her head high and her eyes on her goal.

"We agreed not to ask where our *relationship* was going." He met her by the back bumper of her car, folded his arms and cocked his head. His tanned face tensed. "But I think 'where ya going?' is a perfectly valid question to be asking when I drop by and find you leaving your house with a suitcase in each hand."

She lifted the smaller piece of luggage and fit it into the trunk. "All my unfinished business is in Atlanta, Travis."

"Not *all* of it," he reminded her, moving closer. He reached out to brush a lock of hair from her cheek. As his finger dragged along the sensitive skin, the soft blond curl wrapped around his knuckle.

Jo inhaled sharp and quick at his touch. When he did not move his hand away, she lowered her lashes and murmured, "I thought as a minister you were on the side of helping people *avoid* temptation."

His gorgeous eyes sparkled. "Temptation?"

"You standing here looking adorable, hinting that there's something more between us and that I should stay and tend to it?" She gave his chest a light push as though shoving off from him, then bent at the knees to reach for the large suitcase still sitting in the drive.

"I don't know about adorable." He smiled. "But I do know this."

She froze, knees bent, hand open above the luggage handle. "What? What do you know, Travis?"

He leaned in again, whispering against her temple so that her blond hair trembled in front of her eyes. "That was no hint."

"No?" She turned her head only slightly, but that was enough to put her eyes just inches from his. "Then what was it?"

"That was a promise."

Her heart pounded so hard she felt it in her knees, her throat, her fingertips and even her lips as she asked, "A promise of what?"

"That there is something between us, Jo." He did not move nearer but somehow his very words brought him so close she could feel the warmth of his breath. "Don't forget you have unfinished business here, too."

Suddenly, warm breath or not, her skin tightened into a thousand tiny chill bumps. She grabbed the handle of her suitcase, gritted her teeth then hoisted it up. She wrestled it into the trunk, practically snorting from the mix of exertion and disenchantment. "Business."

His feet never moved. He angled his shoulder back and opened his arms in resignation. "Bad word choice."

"But exactly the right word for what stands between us and, well, finding the right words, as it were." She readjusted the cases until they fit so snugly against each other that the drive wouldn't budge them. "You were right about that. I have so much business to attend to, personal issues and professional, that I can't do anything else until I've taken care of that."

He nodded. "When are you leaving?"

"First thing in the morning." She gave the back of her car a quick check to make sure she had everything. "I want to make sure Billy J is all right and not just run out on my mom and sisters."

"How long will you be gone?"

"As long as it takes." Jo reached for the trunk lid.

Travis beat her to it.

Their fingers brushed and his hand fit over hers.

Jo looked up and met his steady, open gaze. She could not say for certain what she hoped to find. Pride in her decision? Encouragement? A silent plea for her not to go?

No, none of those rightly captured the simple need in her.

She wanted . . .

He shut the trunk.

She wanted him not to just look at her, but to *see* her. She wanted him to acknowledge how much it had taken for her to make this first step. How far she had come already toward becoming the person she *could* be.

He studied her a moment.

"Any other questions?" she asked, secretly hoping the next thing out of his mouth would tell her everything that she wanted to know.

"Yes."

Ask me if I'll miss you. Ask me if I will come back to you. Ask me if I love you.

"Why are you doing this now?"

Jo stood there, stunned.

He might as well have asked, "Who on earth *are* you?"

"Are you doing this because I told you to? Because you see it as a condition of you and I pursuing a relationship? Or are you—"

"If you must know, I'm doing it now because . . ."

Because she could not recognize herself in the

135

picture of her family in the paper. Because while she had talked a big plan of helping local women, she didn't have the emotional, financial or street credibility to do so with her life in shreds. Because she made footprints in the sand that vanished at the first gentle wash of an incoming wave.

"I'm doing it now because today when Moxie got mad about everyone closing in on her at the Urgent Care Clinic, I realized that I was the one person who had no reason to actually be there. Nobody expected it of me, nobody needed anything from me."

"Jo, you have to realize how important a part you play in everyone's—"

"You don't have to try to make me feel better about that, Travis."

"I don't?" He didn't even try to hide his relief or show any embarrassment over the fact that she'd caught him outright trying to mollify her.

"No. Not anymore." She looked at the cottage then at the car where she had just placed her suitcases, then at him. "As I stood there fighting off my inclination to feel sorry for myself I couldn't help comparing my situation to others around me and realizing how blessed I am."

"Blessed?"

"For all the times I have struggled with jealousy of my older *and*—in one form or another—of my baby sister, right now I have the one thing Kate

136

has always wanted and Moxie is now demanding."

"I don't know what you're talking about," he admitted.

"Freedom," she said.

"Freedom?" he asked, still openly confused by it all.

"The choice about what I do with my life is in my own hands." She held them out.

He looked down at her open palms as though he almost expected to find the answers to his questions there.

"Don't you see, Travis? Right now, with Kate in no position to ditch Mom and finally promising not to pull the Scat-Kat Katie routine again and me without any commitments here, now is the time to do what I should have done months ago but was too self-involved to try."

"Go back to Atlanta?"

"Atlanta is only the first step," she told him, feeling more sure of herself than she had in a very longtime. Sure enough to speak aloud the thing she planned, the thing she hoped for, the thing that would finally make her her own woman, capable of finally following her dreams instead of hiding behind her fears. "I'm going to stand on my own two feet."

Chapter Thirteen

Kate fell, exhausted, onto the comfy old over-stuffed couch in the front room of the cottage and shut her eyes. Rest, not sleep, was what she was after.

Rest from the prickly thread of tension that had run through her lifetime between herself and Jo and their mother. Rest from the new, even more prickly tension winding its way between all of them and Moxie. Rest from her worries about her commitment to stay in Santa Sofia and start a new business. Rest from the back-and-forth of her emotions about Vince and their future.

Will he ask me, won't he ask me? She felt that a ten-year-old with her first crush, plucking petals from a daisy, had a better chance of discerning a useful answer than she did. Maybe if she asked him delicately? Wheedled him? Manipulated him ever so slightly and in the sweetest, most well-intentioned way? Or out-and-out issued him an ultimatum?

No. She knew better than that. She had a model for what it meant to love one another. Opening her eyes, she reached for her mother's Bible, which she kept on the table to read from each evening. The well-worn book fell open to the New Testament and Kate only had to flip a few pages to find 1 Corinthians, Chapter 13.

"Love is patient. Love is kind. It does not envy. It does not boast. It is not proud. It is not rude. It is not self-seeking." That pretty much gave Kate her answer about trying to maneuver a proposal from Vince.

She read on. "It is not easily angered. It keeps no record of wrongs."

No record of wrongs. How much stronger, deeper, much more meaningful would all her relationships be if she applied that tenet to them? She thought of how she had punished herself since childhood for feeling she had not done enough to rescue Molly Christina. Of how Jo could never let go of her anger and her sense of being wronged and unloved because their father had left her behind and their mother and Kate had not needed her enough.

"Love does not delight in evil but rejoices with the truth. It always protects, always trusts, always hopes, always perseveres." Kate looked up. Protects, trusts, hopes, perseveres. Were those words anyone would use to describe good ol' Scat-Kat Kate over the years? Hardly.

She read on silently until she came to the conclusion of the chapter. "And now these three remain: faith, hope and love. But the greatest of these is love."

Even as she took comfort in the message, her thoughts tumbled over one another. So much had happened since they moved down here, yet so little had changed.

She glanced around the room that remained much as it had all those years ago when they came here for vacation. The pattern on the floral couch where she now sat had faded and worn almost threadbare in spots. The coffee table had a few more nicks in the edge and one of the legs wobbled if you put too much weight on that side. The coarse plaid upholstery, earth tones circa 1974, of the couch across the coffee table showed little sign of age. That, in and of itself, dated the thing. The fabric must have been made from some industrial strength synthetic not unlike the polyester pants suits her mom kept hanging in the closet, "just in case they come back in style some day."

"Trust me, Mom, these are never going to come back in style," she could hear perfectionist Jo assuring the pragmatic and sometimes penny-pinching Dodie.

Sometimes penny-pinching? Kate gave her collar a shake to create a stir of air over her neck. She wanted to go crank the air-conditioning up but knew it would only bring the wrath of Dodie down on her head.

She shut her eyes and told herself not to think about the rising heat and humidity. She kicked off her lone shoe, wriggled the toes on her one uninjured foot and sighed, feeling cooler despite knowing that the temperature had not dropped a fraction of a degree.

If only she could shut out the constant chaos in her heart and mind so easily. If only . . .

"This house is too quiet." Dodie pulled aside the dingy old curtain to peer out the front window, sighed then let it fall shut again.

Kate did not open her eyes. "Well, Mom, you were the one who wanted to move down here and live in our vacation cottage full-time."

"Yes, but when I first came up with that idea, I expected some friends would move down here with me." She came to the couch and plopped down on the end opposite Kate. "And then—"

Kate held her hand up to cut her mother off. She peered through one eye at her getting-grubbier-by-the-minute cast. "I *know* what happened next."

One hospital stay, two surgeries, numerous doctors and countless bills later, Jo got the brilliant plan to come to their old vacation home for a long, uneventful recovery.

Except when had anything the Cromwell women tried to do in life been uneventful? She placed her hand on her forehead.

"I was going to say, then you girls found your true loves down here and decided to stay." Dodie

141

shifted her weight. The couch groaned then jostled Kate like a wave as the cushions redistributed their bulk.

Clunk. Clunk. Thump.

"Ahhhh."

Kate did not have to look to know Dodie's bargain shoes, the ones that did not quite fit—"but for that price, you squeeze your toes in and hope the uppers stretch"—hit the floor. Then her feet came up to rest on the battered coffee table.

"You have, haven't you?" Dodie asked at last, sounding physically contented and comfortable but emotionally tentative.

That was a sound Kate knew by heart. In fact, she thought, that was the closest her mother ever came to sounding actually happy since the night Molly Christina had disappeared from their lives.

"Have what, Mom?" Kate knew what her mother was driving at but she wanted to play it out. Of course, Dodie wanted to know if Vince had proposed. Or, barring that, at least if Travis had made his intentions clear to Jo. Kate smiled. Some of the things that did not change gave her great peace of mind, she decided. A bit of maternal nosiness was one of those things. "Found our true loves?"

"Decided to stay put, Scat-Kat Katie." The contentment all but left her mother's voice and apprehension subdued it to a quiet murmur.

Suddenly Kate's head hurt. She winced and turned her face away. "Mom, I asked you not to call me that."

"That's not an answer." Dodie gave Kate's ankle a nudge with her bare toe.

"It's not as though she has moved back to Atlanta. As soon as she gets her money issues sorted out there, she'll be back."

"I wasn't asking you to speak for Jo, Kate."

Kate. Not Scat-Kat Katie. She felt she had to dignify that concession with an answer. And she had one.

If she ever hoped to walk without a cane again, she would need at least two more surgeries. That meant more hospital time, a lot of recovery time and loads more bills. More bills meant she had to keep making money and the only way to do that was to honor her commitment to Lionel and the Urgent Care Clinic.

Yes, Gentry and Pera were taking Fabbie and moving to Miami. That very well meant that Vince might pick up and follow his family. *His* family.

Not hers.

Kate's family was all here in Santa Sofia—or would eventually be when Jo came back. Unless Vince did something to change the definition of what Kate considered constituted her family, this was where she belonged. Even if he did ask . . . well, she'd have to think about that later.

"Mom, as far as I know, I'm not going anywhere."

"That's all I wanted to hear." She gave Kate's leg a pat and sprang up from the couch.

Kate's eyes flew open in time to see her go clip-clopping toward the kitchen, trying to wriggle her feet into her too-small shoes as she went. "Where are you going?"

Dodie snatched up the car keys and her handbag. "See you later!"

"But, when will you—"

The slamming back door cut her off.

Kate tried to lumber up to her feet but the propped-up position of her injured foot hampered any speedy movement. "Wait a minute! Come back here! It's not right that you make me promise not to leave Santa Sofia then just up and—"

"Going someplace, Kate?" The back door swung open and a large, dark figure stepped into the brightly lit kitchen.

"Vince! What, are you in cahoots with my mom about something?"

"Cahoots?" He snorted a laugh and came into the front room, smelling of Florida sunshine, his hair windswept and his eyes gleaming. "Next I guess you'll ask me if I'm getting up to some kind of crazy shenanigans."

"I would never ask any such thing!" she protested.

"Yeah?" He looked down at her, his smile hinting at piqued curiosity as he demanded to know, "Why not?"

"Because I always know that if you ever got up to any crazy shenanigans, I wouldn't *have* to ask you about them. I'd be right there beside you knee-deep in the mayhem."

He laughed. "Now that is the measure of a true friend."

Friend? Was that how he thought of her? She wanted to ask but since she couldn't say for sure that she wanted to hear the answer, she pushed herself up into a more upright position and asked instead, "Did you see my mom as you came in? Do you know what she's up to? And if you don't, would you please run out there to see if you can catch her and—"

"Not much point in that." He lifted his head as if listening.

Nothing. No car engine. No tires on the gravel drive.

Vince shook his head. "You mom is long gone."

Kate laid her head back and covered her eyes with one hand. "Sometimes I think my mom was long gone before she ever even arrived!"

"Give her a break. She's in a hurry to go see Billy J."

"Billy J? I thought they were running tests. Moxie asked that we stay clear until they finished."

"Yep, she called me earlier today and gave the all-clear."

"Called *you?*"

He nodded. "And I called your mom."

"When?"

"Half an hour ago." He picked his way around the coffee table then sat gingerly beside her, careful not to jar her foot. "She told me then she planned to take off to see him as soon as I could get here."

"Get here?" Kate pointed to the floor beneath them. "She asked you to come over and do what? Babysit me?"

"She didn't hire me as a babysitter, Kate. She just didn't want to leave you stranded. I just didn't think you'd mind a couple hours alone with me."

"Oh, no. That's great. I just . . ."

"What?"

She couldn't confess what she suspected—that her mother had gotten her to promise to stay in Santa Sofia because she knew Vince was on his way over. Mom knew about the situation with Gentry and his job. She knew Vince thought the world of his son and granddaughter, and might just be tempted to tag along if the young family moved to Miami.

Dodie had to fear that, given the choice, Kate would never let Vince go again.

What her mother didn't know was that Kate

wasn't convinced she actually *had* Vince or that if he left, he'd ask her to come, too.

"Never mind. It was sweet of her, I suppose, in a very Dodie-esque way." She smiled at him. "So what's the news on Gentry's job offer?"

Vince laced his fingers in his lap and cast his gaze down. "He and Pera want to go to Miami for a weekend to see if they even want to live there before he accepts any offers."

She wanted to go to him, put her arms around his neck and tell him not to borrow trouble by assuming his son and beloved grandchild would move away for certain. But she couldn't move. For once Scat-Kat Katie couldn't move.

And she certainly couldn't offer advice about not borrowing trouble to anyone, not where family was concerned.

She let her shoulders sink back into the softness of a cushion and exhaled slowly. "When will they have time to go to Miami before the job is filled?"

"They won't." He rubbed his hand up the back of his neck, still not meeting her eyes as he said, "Not unless they go this weekend."

"*This* weekend?" That was fast. This was all happening *so fast.* She felt she'd just gotten her chance at love at long last and now it could all slip away. "As in two days from now?"

He nodded, moved his hand around to rub his knuckles under his chin and stared across the room. "They want me to watch Fabbie."

"They do?"

She hated to seem skeptical, but Gentry and his wife had had a very stormy relationship up until a couple of months ago when Kate had come to town and played a part in helping Gentry accept his role as the man of the family. Until then Vince had made it easy for his son to avoid his responsibilities. He'd made excuses for him, bailed him out financially and generally allowed him to remain a kid for far too long. Pera knew all these things.

She knew that without Vince's enabling, Gentry might have worked harder to make their marriage work from the very start instead of seeing it as one more thing he could walk away from if it proved too hard. It might even be a reason one of her own relatives had suddenly turned up with a job offer, to create space between father and son and make a place for their own little family to flourish.

Pera loved Vince. But she knew he had spoiled Gentry almost to the point of ruining his life. Of course, she wouldn't think the man could do the same for Fabbie in a couple of days, but Kate had a hard time thinking she'd reward him for his past transgressions by setting a precedent of him taking the child on his own for extended stays.

"Are you sure about that? You're going to watch Fabbie by yourself for a whole weekend?"

"Sure they . . . No." He finally looked up at her and grinned sheepishly. "Actually, Pera wants to take Fabbie with them, but Gentry feels like they won't get as much done with the baby along."

"Get as much done with the baby along?" She folded her arms. "Did he have a little gleam in his eyes when he said that?"

"Absolutely." Vince laughed. "Maybe if everything works out, I'll have a second grandchild to babysit soon enough."

Kate laughed, too, only not with her whole heart. A second grandbaby. Another reason for him not to stay in Santa Sofia. Or, if he did stay, for him not to need any further distractions from his family obligations.

"Anyway, the way Gentry sees it, they aren't really leaving Fabbie with me alone. They're leaving her with us."

"Us?"

"Oh, yeah, didn't I tell you that part yet?" He put his arm around her.

"Oh, no."

"What?"

"You are up to some crazy shenanigans!"

"And you're up to them right there with me, Kate." He gave her a squeeze. "I hope."

If she had any sense, she'd push his arm away, hoist herself up off this couch and storm off to teach him that he couldn't just assume she would go along with whatever he promised people on their behalf. Not unless he put a ring on her finger first.

And even then he'd still better ask her first before making a weekend-long commitment for her.

Either she didn't have any sense or the old Scat-Kat had begun to fade for certain. Because Kate did not fly off the handle or even scootch over an inch on the couch. She snuggled close, tipped her head so that she could look into Vince's eyes and said softly, "I'm listening. What didn't you not tell me yet?"

"The only way Pera will agree to going away is if she knows you're helping to take care of Fabbie."

"Doesn't trust Grandpa not to spoil the kid rotten?"

"She's seen my handiwork with Gentry. I have a reputation of being a little indulgent."

Kate smiled. It was good to hear him admit it. "And it's good to see Gentry trying to let go of Fabbie just a little."

"Yeah. I think that's healthy."

"Me, too."

"He's setting a good example." *For you.* She didn't say it but she didn't have to. "I know this is tough, to see him considering moving so far away."

"I know the job of a parent is to give your kid wings, but Miami sure is a far-off place for him to fly."

"Look on the bright side. Maybe they won't like it." The second the words came flying out, she slapped her hand over her mouth. Too late, of course. But if her renewed relationship with Vince had taught her anything, it was . . .

Hmm. What *had* she learned from falling head over heels in love with Vince again?

Kate lowered her hand slowly.

Love. She *loved* Vince.

And Fabbie.

And Gentry and Pera.

And her mother and sisters.

And she wanted all the best for them, no matter what. That meant putting her own desires and fears aside.

And now these three remain: faith, hope and love. But the greatest of these is love.

"Okay. You can count on me. I'll help you take care of Fabbie this weekend." What happened after that, she'd leave up to the Lord.

Chapter Fourteen

The bell over the door at the *Santa Sofia Sun Times* jingled to announce Moxie's arrival at ten minutes after nine.

Clink-clunk. Clink-clunk.

As a local business person she'd heard the dented brass bell hundreds of times. Thousands, maybe. But never before had she felt it resonate through her.

Clink-clunk. Clink-clunk.

It was the sound her anxious but wary heart would make if it were a bell. Her cheeks flushed at the sheer corniness—and dead-on accuracy of the description—of her response to crossing the threshold into the office of R. Hunt Diamante.

Call me Hunt.

"Hunt," she whispered at the recollection of his request. She had come to see Hunt today. On business, of course, and she was . . . puzzled.

Puzzled and alone.

The *Sun Times* had occupied the same building forever. Well, Moxie remembered the offices here forever, it seemed. Or at least since third grade when an elementary-school field trip made her aware that the neat little bundle that arrived on the doorstep every morning came out of an office in Santa Sofia and was written by citizens of the town.

Not much had changed about it since then. Not outwardly. Venetian blinds still hung in the plate-glass window, casting slatted shadows over the pocked but polished wooden floors of the lobby. The receptionist's area was still not much more than a square hole cut in the paneled wall. All sorts of awards, commendations, subscription rates, photos of Little League teams the paper had sponsored and the old journalistic adage Never Assume in plastic and metal frames covered the wall. Even though bits of the gold paint had chipped away the dots on both of the *i*'s and at a good portion of the *u, Santa Sofia Sun Times* was still on the front door in Old English script. Whenever the news or the so-called reporting of it got too bad for locals to handle, they liked to point out the missing bits of the *u,* which made the letter look like an *i,* without a dot—like the other *i*'s in the name— and make the same old corny joke.

"Went down to complain to the *Sun Times* about their paper and found they'd changed the name to the Sin Times and figured I better not get caught hanging out around a place like that!"

Maybe it wasn't just a joke, Moxie found herself wondering. Maybe nobody came down to the

Sun Times offices anymore. But Hunt still worked here.

Didn't he?

"Hello?" she shouted into the stillness of the dusty old office.

Nothing.

No shuffling of feet from the unseen back offices toward the front. No clackity-clack of fingers running over a keyboard. No phone ringing. No human voices chatting to each other, much less calling out to her that someone would be right with her.

"Peg?" she called out for the woman who had worked at the *Sun Times* since—as Peg herself liked to put it—since we hammered the headlines into stone tablets with a rock and a bone chisel. "Peg? Y'all in the back? If you're in a meeting, I can come back."

No answer.

Moxie took a step closer to the unoccupied front desk, aka the hole in the paneling. She opened her mouth to call out again then paused, unsure *what* exactly to call out.

Peg clearly was not here.

She knew the other reporters, sort of, but not on a first-name basis. If she did call to one of them and they showed up, what would she say? That she wanted to see Hunt?

Moxie drew in a deep breath then leaned in, trying to peer through the opening in the wall.

The lights were on. The computer, off. The red light on the answering machine blinking.

This all felt so wrong. *Spooky.*

Except Moxie did not believe in spooks. She pretty much figured most odd or mysterious events had a perfectly reasonable man-made solution. Her own life story seemed evidence of that.

Still, the empty office did set her nerves on edge. She strode forward and reached out to pick up the phone. Maybe she should call—

R-r-r-r-r-ring.

Moxie just about jumped out of her skin. Her heart thumped hard and fast in the hollow of her throat.

R-r-r-r-r-ring.

By the second ring she had calmed down enough to realize this call might offer some insight into what was going on around here. Or at least it would give her someone else to help try to piece things together.

R-r-r-

Wham.

Boom. Boom. Boom.

A door somewhere in the back of the building slammed shut. Heavy footsteps falling in long, running strides drowned out the last jingle of the phone.

A muffled, "Yeah, what is it?"

Moxie tipped her head, more trying to confirm

155

the identity of the speaker than to listen in on the content of the conversation.

"I can't answer that . . . No. No. I can't . . . I don't know . . . Look, I'm sorry, lady, but I gotta go . . . Yeah. Yeah. You do that . . . Okay. All right . . . Thanks . . . Goodbye."

A moment of silence followed by a mild but descriptive curse word.

"Hunt?" As she called his name, she stretched up on her tiptoes as if that would give her voice the extra oomph it needed to reach the man and let him know she was there. "Is something wrong? Is there anything I can do to help?"

"I've never been so happy to hear anyone's voice in my life!"

Moxie couldn't help but smile. It wasn't a profession of love, or even like, which was the most appropriate level of affection either of them should feel toward the other given the short amount of time they had known one another and the circumstances of their, well, circumstances.

He was happy to hear her voice. That was enough for now.

"I'm just so glad you came back, Peg." He came to a stop, looked around, then laced his arms defensively over his puffed-up chest. "You're not Peg."

"I'm not Maxine, either, though you have called me that." Her smile went from high beam to fog lights to completely off in the length of time it

156

took her to complete that sentence.

"They did it." He strode to the door, opened it, looked to the north, then to the south, then directly across the street. "They actually did it."

"Who did what?" she asked, following his line of vision.

He frowned. Then, still totally distracted, he turned and headed for the door that led to the back offices.

Moxie didn't know what else to do but follow. "Whatever is going on here, I'd like to help."

He came to a halt beside the receptionist's office and finally fixed his gaze fully on her face. His harried expression softened slightly. "I believe that, Moxie."

"Good." She took a deep breath. A connection, at last.

He spun on his heel and marched into the small cubicle where Peg usually sat greeting people and directing phone calls.

Again, Moxie followed. "But I can't help with anything if I don't know what's going on."

He frowned at Peg's desk.

She moved in front of him, glanced at the desk and found it so clear of paper that she didn't think it would hurt for her to hop up and sit on it.

Hunt didn't so much as blink at her seating choice.

That he accepted the fact that she felt so comfortable in his new domain made her feel good.

She folded her hands with a clap in her lap, crossed her legs at the ankle, then let them swing just a little. "Okay, so tell me. Who are *they* and just what did they actually *do?*"

"The newspaper staff."

"Randall, Joyce, Mel and—"

"And Peg. Yeah." He laid his finger on the patch of beard along his chin.

The gesture, along with the deepening lines in his forehead, made him look lost in thought. A man weighing his options, considering his next move.

She studied his somber, dark eyes made darker by the circles beneath them. He hadn't been sleeping well. The pallor of his usually rich olive skin told her he probably hadn't eaten well, either. It didn't hurt that conclusion that she'd seen the greasy junk he had piled on his plate at the Bait Shack.

This was not a man who acted on impulse. Not a man ruled by emotions. When he had gotten out of the car or offered to take her father to the hospital, that had come from who he was, not how he felt about her or her father or the situation. He saw what needed to be done and responded. Now he was trying to formulate the proper response to this new predicament. It obviously had no clear-cut right answer.

"Hunt?"

"Hmm?"

"What did they do?" She repeated the question without a trace of impatience.

His whole face pinched; he rubbed his temple and shook his head. "They walked out on me."

Moxie let out a long, low whistle.

He chuckled at that, then added quietly, "Thanks."

"For what?"

"Not immediately asking me 'what did you do to deserve that?'"

Moxie smiled. "Every story has more than one side. Surely you've learned that as a journalist."

He nodded in appreciation. "And I guess you've learned it by having your life story butchered by a so-called journalist?"

"Hmm. I hadn't thought about that. I'd have said I learned it in my work in property management."

"Ah!"

"*And* from living my life's story. Not the version in the *Sun Times*, by the way. Each member of my family has his or her take on what happened to this point and has their own opinions about what should happen next."

"Don't get me started on family." He turned then sat on the edge of the desk and rubbed his hands over his face.

"Started? I don't even know *how* to start talking about family. Up until I reconnected with the Cromwells the only family I had to cope with was my dad and a foster mother who didn't really want to be any kind of mother."

"Tough going."

"I guess. It made me who I am, though, so there's that."

He gave a short, empathetic snort. "That's one way of dealing with a . . . um . . . unique family dynamic."

"Unique? Kidnapped baby raised by kindly strangers within miles of birth family's vacation home? That's so common Hallmark has its own section in the Mother's Day cards for it."

He laughed outright. "I meant my unique family."

"Oh?"

"Yeah."

"No, not 'oh' as in 'oh, I get it.' 'Oh' followed by a big, fat question mark." She drew the punctuation in the air to, well, *punctuate* her comment. "Or, as my decidedly more Southern-sounding sisters and birth mother might say, 'do tell!' "

Another laugh, accompanied by a shake of his head. "I have enough to deal with, what with my whole staff walking out. I don't have the time or the energy to go into some sad old song and dance about the black sheep struggling to prove himself to . . . well, you know."

She didn't know and she *wanted* to, but clearly he didn't feel like going into details. Moxie sighed and pushed herself up and off the desk.

"Okay, I get it. You're preoccupied. Too pre-occupied to do a little business?"

"Business?"

"I promised to run an ad in the next issue of the *Sun Times*, remember?"

He placed the heels of his hands on the edge of the desk and braced his arms straight on either side of his body. He didn't budge from the spot where he was leaning back to rest. "Much as I appreciate you keeping your promise, I can't do the same with my staff gone. I can't promise I'll even get an issue out this week."

"Oh, surely they'll come back."

"I don't know. They were awfully mad."

Moxie bit her lower lip.

He narrowed his eyes at her. "You want to ask, don't you?"

She squirmed.

He started to smile, reined it in, then let it ease over his lips.

He sure was awfully cute when he smiled.

"Okay." He shut his eyes and chuckled softly. "Ask."

How could she phrase this delicately? She scooted close enough to press her shoulder to his, then leaned forward to look at him square in the eye. "What did you do to make them mad enough to walk out?"

He drew in a deep breath. His eyes darted to one side for only a second before his gaze locked on hers. The weight of his problems showed in his posture, his expression, even his deep, weary tone, and he exhaled slowly then shook his head. "I told them the truth."

Chapter Fifteen

"Ad revenues? That's what this is all about?"

"Not *all* about. It's not *that* simple." He stood and strode across the room and into the hallway. He looked down it first one way and then the next, gesturing with both hands as he said, "Cost of paper is up. Cost of production. Electricity. Water. Gas for delivery."

"All things the *Sun Times* newspaper staff would totally understand." She pushed up off the desk and followed him as far as the doorway. There she stopped, folded her arms and cocked her head and challenged him. "I can't believe they'd walk out over hearing a few cold, hard facts."

He scrunched up his face like a kid caught trying to get away with not having told the whole story. "Yeah, well, maybe it wasn't just the facts that were cold and hard."

"You have my attention."

"I just . . . I didn't intend to say it. Not the way it came out." He pretended to pick at something on the paneled hallway wall, then leaned against it, his arm straight and his palm flat. "But the longer we sat in the staff meeting trouble-shooting—"

"Troubleshooting?" Moxie held her hand up to stop him right there. "You mean problem solving?"

He let his arm go lax, just a tiny bit. That put his face closer to hers, not in a threatening way but in a way that implied he did not like being corrected and he didn't plan to back off his original phrasing. "Troubleshooting. Problem solving. Same thing."

"I beg to differ, Mr. Editor in chief."

He dropped his hand from the wall and stood with his shoulders back and his expression skeptical but not closed off. "I'm listening."

"Troubleshooting means you are looking for trouble, usually with a double-barreled rifle loaded with buckshot approach."

He tipped his head momentarily to the right. It wasn't a nod of agreement, but it let her know he was on board with her theory and willing to hear more.

"Problem solving, on the other hand, means you know what the issues are and you are looking for resolutions, looking for a way to get out of trouble."

"I never thought of it that way." Then he rubbed the bent knuckle of his index finger over his narrow beard and chuckled, his eyes narrowed onto her face. "You always this smart?"

"No." Moxie didn't know why she immediately denied it. There was nothing wrong with a girl being smart and Moxie was. Then again, if she kept to the absolute truth, she wasn't always smart. And frankly, this man could come up with recent and very vivid examples of her, um, lack of intellect. "But I have run my own businesses since I was sixteen years old. I picked up a thing or two along the way."

"Sixteen. Wow. When I was sixteen . . ." He stared off into space, shook his head then asked, "So where were your parents then? Were you supporting yourself?"

"My foster mom had just left. Billy J was a wreck—yes, even more so than he is now." She answered the obvious question before he could even pose it.

He laughed, then added, "I don't know him well, but from what I do know, I like the man."

"Me, too," she said softly. "Of course, I love him, but I also like him. You know what I mean?"

More staring off into the distance, his dark eyebrows furrowed. "Not everyone can say that about their family. They love them but they also like them."

She considered delving into the wistfulness behind that statement then decided a man not swayed by emotion who had already told her more than she suspected he planned to might find that kind of question too intrusive.

165

"To answer your question—" she directed the conversation away from his issues "—I had a great home and the whole town of Santa Sofia looking out for me. And the Bait Shack provided more than enough financial security."

"I noticed that with all the economic downturn around here, it still seems pretty busy."

"People have to eat," she said. "They come from all over, and tourists still think it's worth their while to get off the highway to eat at the Bait Shack. It's a sort of landmark. My dad's success helps the whole town."

"And a newspaper, for example, should be different because . . . ?"

"Because it *can* be," she told him.

"And the business you've been in since you were a kid?"

"I help people put a roof over their heads, make a home. Those that have problems realizing that dream, I work with. I serve the community as much as I can, *because* I can."

"And therefore you should."

"Don't give me that tone, not from a guy who played the—" she pulled her shoulders up, put on a somber scowl and pretended to stroke an imaginary Pharaoh-like beard "'—I am taking you to the hospital because it's the right thing to do not because you're taking out an ad' card."

"All right. All right." He laughed and held up

166

both hands. "Guilty. You're all about the altruism and I'm a diehard capitalist."

"Look, Hunt, I am just a good person trying to live my faith."

He did not flinch. "I understand."

"Really?"

"I may not qualify as a poster boy for the church-going crowd but I am a man of faith, Moxie."

She got the feeling he did not say that out loud often. Not out of shame but because he was the kind who didn't think you should have to proclaim it for people to know it.

"I'm hardly a shining example all the time myself." That made Moxie want to come clean. "And as for my business being all about altruism? I went into business for myself because I'd figured out that summer that no matter how much money or how many kind folks you have in your life, basically, a person has to learn to rely on themselves. So I wasn't supporting myself so much as I was taking care of myself."

"That's a pretty harsh lesson for a sixteen-year-old to take."

"I guess you're never too old to learn something new. I'm trying to do that, especially where my new family is concerned."

He studied her in silence.

She squirmed, shifting her weight from one foot to the other. "What?"

"Nothing. Just thinking that I want to be like you when I grow up."

"You look like a man fully growed to me," she teased, then felt her cheeks burning. She hadn't meant that as flirtatious as it had come out. "I mean, you're clearly adult, mature, responsible."

He laughed. "Yeah. Tell that to my family."

"Family." She shook her head.

"Yeah. It's because of them, because of my family, I said what I did. It's their philosophy. Not mine. Well, maybe it's mine. I thought it was, now I just don't know."

"Well, I certainly don't know. Maybe it would help if you'd tell me what you're talking about."

"I'm talking about what I said to the staff. What I told them that made them walk out."

Moxie held her hand out to coax him to spill it.

His shoulders rose and fell. He shook his head then exhaled and straightened his back as he faced her and said, "I told them that all media is first and foremost a business."

"Really? Not even a passing reference to the nobility of the fourth estate? To the duty of the free press to inform the public, shine a light on injustice and wrongdoing?"

"Some people would say that the only form of media that does that anymore is the hero of a graphic novel."

"I think there are plenty of people who would disagree with that, from Miz Nancy who runs the

Christian bookstore down the road to the local talk radio station to your very own newspaper staff."

He huffed at the mention of his wayward workforce.

Moxie went on, undeterred. "I'd say they all could cite examples of how different forms of media have helped people, changed lives even."

"Look, I was just trying to tell it to them straight," he huffed. "I don't know for sure how things work in Santa Sofia, but I'm guessing the banks around here won't let you write a check on the satisfaction of having championed a noble cause."

She hesitated then conceded his point with a halfhearted shrug and a nod.

"No matter the goal, none of it can happen if the media doesn't make a profit, right?"

Another nod.

"For a newspaper, that profit comes from ad revenues first and to some degree sales and subscriptions. I told my staff that."

"Which they obviously knew all along, so—"

"And then I added the proverbial last straw. Something that might as well be my family's motto." He looked away from her. "Media accomplishes more by gaining affluence than by giving insight."

"Wow." Moxie tried to process all that and found herself torn between disagreeing with that premise with all her might and with asking him, "That's your family philosophy? Media exists to make a profit, not to serve the community?"

"*Everything* exists to make a profit. If it doesn't . . ." He jerked his thumb over his shoulder in the classic sign for throwing a player out of the ball game.

"And the *Sun Times* isn't making enough of a profit, so according to your upbringing . . . ?" She repeated his gesture.

He didn't confirm anything, just said matter-of-factly, "Something has to give. Rates have to go up."

"You'd have the whole town on your doorstep complaining."

"Complaints I could take. The landslide of canceled subscriptions, that would make the few advertisers we have left walk? That I can't accept."

"What about cutbacks?"

"As of this hour, staff's down to just me." He held both hands out, his arms wide to showcase his singularity. "That might help."

"They'll come back after they cool down."

"Then what do I do? Ask them all to take a pay cut or to decide among themselves which one I fire?"

She saw his point. "What if you just get more advertisers?"

"I've been all over town. Everybody says they'll take an ad next week, next month, next . . . editor." He looked like a lost pup as he said that.

"Aww." Moxie stuck her lower lip out in a show of sympathy. "You think it's personal?"

"Don't you?"

She thought about it a moment then shook her head. "I think it's regional."

"What?"

She smiled, quite pleased with herself that she had, at that instant, done a little problem solving of her own and had a solution in mind that just might turn things around. "It's a Southern thing."

"Are you saying they won't take ads out with me because I'm a Yankee?"

Moxie laughed. "To quote someone I have recently come to admire, it's not that simple."

"You admire me?"

"Better than that," she replied. "I see potential in you."

"To do what?"

"Grow up to be like me." She gave him a pat on the arm and turned to head toward the lobby. "If you ever hope to accomplish that *and* problem solve about how to be the kind of paper your staff and this town needs, not to mention put yourself in good stead with the local advertisers, you have to start where I did."

"The Cromwells?" He took a tentative step behind her.

"No, silly." She gave him a look over her shoulder, reached for the door and swung it open for him to pass through. "Billy J's Bait Shack Seafood Buffet. Where you are going to get a lesson in service that will serve *you* well for the rest of your life."

Chapter Sixteen

Jo stepped through the door of Mike Powers Realty, shut her eyes and sighed. It felt like slipping into a pair of custom-fit ridiculously high-priced Italian pumps. It pinched a little and had almost no practical application in her real life, but, man, she looked great doing it.

"Jo!"

"You're back!"

"Love your hair short like that!"

"Florida living looks good on you, girl!"

Jo acknowledged every greeting and comment but she did not let them deter her from her objective. She had come here to clean up the mess she'd made of her finances in the name of ambition. There was no way to do that without directly confronting . . .

"Jo Cromwell, Super Realtor!"

"Mike?" She jerked to a halt.

"The prodigal has returned."

Prodigal? Jo hugged her handbag close, her shoulders high. She took a step back. Is that what Mike thought of her? That she had run off to Florida to squander money and misbehave, leaving him and everyone here to take up the slack at work? That was so far from the truth she didn't know what to say, except, "I'm hardly a prodigal."

"Oh? You are all *churchy,* though. Prodigal, that's from the Bible, right?"

"Yes, but . . ."

"I knew it. I've sat through a few Sunday-school classes in my life. After taking off and living it up for a while, when the prodigal came back, everybody celebrated!"

"Well, not *everybody* celebrated," she corrected him, thinking of the son who had held a grudge against his returning brother. Is that how Mike felt? Did he really believe she had gone off to "live it up"? She opened her mouth to ask him directly, but he had stopped listening to anything but the bark of his own orders.

"Kelley, order pizza!" He stabbed a finger in the direction of his administrative assistant. Then twisted around to the row of desks in the large main office. "Brittney S.? Brittney B.?"

"Yes, sir!" Two almost indistinguishable twenty-somethings jumped up from their seats. Their eager eyes fixed on the charismatic businessman who signed their paychecks. They didn't even try to hide the fact that they thought Mike "hung the moon"—as Dodie would say to describe that level of blatant adoration.

"Call Beakman's Bakery and order a great big chocolate . . ." He turned and looked at Jo questioningly.

Jo tried to show him she had no idea what he was actually asking her by raising her hands and shaking her head.

"Right! Too messy." He turned to the girls again. "Yellow cake, white icing. A big one." He spread his hands apart to indicate the proper size. "Sheet cake."

The girls nodded.

One paused and turned to look at him with her purse raised.

"Please don't spend a dime for my sake," Jo urged Mike, even though her message was aimed at the girl. *Don't let this slick-talking man push you into putting the cost of this totally unwarranted celebration on your credit card with the promise of reimbursement at a later date.* "I'd feel terrible knowing anyone had used her expense account on my account."

Mike paused. His cool expression seemed to hide a thought process that Jo could not quite discern.

Had he caught on that she was projecting her own issues about how he had manipulated her into financing their supposedly "joint" business venture onto the young women? Or maybe he was calculating how much it would cost compared to how much he expected to gain from whatever scheme he had brewing behind that smooth, flawless smile of his.

"Get some money out of petty cash." He pointed to his administrative assistant's impressive desk, which sat just outside his office door.

Brittney S. followed through on Mike's directive and reported to his assistant with her handout.

"Don't skimp," he told the woman looking to him for confirmation that he genuinely meant for her to dole out cold, hard cash. "Oh, and Brittney?"

"Yes?" Both girls looked up.

"Make sure they write on top of it in great big swirly letters." He raised his hands, fingers spread wide and wriggling to emphasize just how expansive and just how swirly he wanted the printing on the cake. "Welcome Home, Jo!"

"Home?" Jo whispered. She had lived in Atlanta since she graduated from college but she did not think she had ever thought of it as home. She certainly would never describe this office with that term. Mike, of all people, knew that.

Jo put her hands on her hips. "Why are you doing this?"

"Because we missed you." He smiled, his arms still extended. "Can't an old friend do a little something special to show how much he missed you and, uh, to say 'good to see you, no hard feelings'?"

Jo shook her head. She wanted to tell him that standing there like that with his perfect brown hair and pearly white teeth and power-red tie he looked more like a smarmy game-show host than a sincere old friend. Instead, she stood her ground and insisted, "If you really want to show me how much you missed me, cake is not the way to do it."

"It's not?"

"You know it's not."

The Brittneys came hurrying back toward him, cash in hand. They looked so pleased and so eager to please the charismatic and commanding Mike Powers.

Jo remembered how that felt. *Felt.* Past tense. Standing here now, she no longer had even an inkling of those old feelings. "If you really want to make amends with me, you can start by putting your intentions in something more permanent than icing."

"Jo, I don't . . . I hope you don't think . . . There's no need for that kind of . . ." He made a series of indefinite gestures to accompany his incomplete thoughts. Then he paused, plastered his practically patented Mike Powers super-salesman grin on his face and cocked his head.

Jo did not budge.

Still smiling, he called out to the girls without taking his eyes off Jo. "Have them put the company logo on that cake, okay?"

"Instead of Welcome Home, Jo?"

"*With* Welcome Home, Jo." His gaze never left Jo's face but some of the falseness fell away from his expression as he said, "Might as well have something we can write off as a business expense. If I like the way this looks, I can use one like it at my next open house. Just some handy knife work and Welcome Home, Jo becomes just plain Welcome Home."

That was more like the Mike she knew. "I'm not coming home, Mike. Atlanta is no longer my home. I just came back to deal with some unfinished business here."

"Oh?"

"So this whole cake idea—"

"I like that. A cake that says Welcome Home at every open house." Mike snapped his fingers at the employee nearest to the door and shouted, "Go after them! Don't have Jo put on the cake. Have the logo the full size of the cake but keep Welcome Home in swirled script."

"Mike, this isn't necessary."

"No, but it's a nice touch for an open house, don't you think? Especially a big one like we have coming up Sunday afternoon." He motioned toward her, then pointed to himself, then her again.

"We? I've been out of state for the past two . . ." She jerked her head up. "What house are you showing Sunday afternoon?"

"Oh, I'm not showing a house. *You* are."

"You can't have scheduled me to show a house this Sunday. Until I called an hour ago and said I was coming in, you thought I was in Florida!"

"Actually I had planned to let the Brittneys take it, but now that you're back, I think you should do the honors, don't you?"

"Honors?" Jo could hardly think of a word less suited to this situation. "There is nothing honorable about all this, Mike. I come back to town to try to get my life in order and minutes after I walk through the door you expect me to start working for you again?"

He tipped his hand to acknowledge her skepticism. "You're not working *just* for me. You stand to benefit from this open house, too, in theory. Not that anyone even comes by for a lookie-loo on that place anymore . . ."

"What place, Mike? Which house are you talking about?"

"Ours, of course."

"Ours?"

"Yeah, you know, the one we bought as partners?"

"I know which house you're talking about." She should—it had practically brought her to the brink of bankruptcy and now it threatened the future she was trying to forge in Santa Sofia. "It's the partnership angle I'm a little hazy on."

"That was always *our* deal, right from the git-go."

"Our deal done on *my* money," she reminded him, giving him her most withering glare.

"Like I said, partners." He gave her a pat and turned away. "Let me know when the cake gets here."

"Mike!" Jo had a very bad feeling about all of this. She hadn't even been by the house yet. She had no idea what kind of shape it was in. "I don't want cake!"

"Why not?"

Because she wanted answers. "Well, for starters I thought you just said you wanted it for Sunday when I'm apparently showing my house."

"*Our* house."

Jo gritted her teeth. Her whole life people had looked past her and done end runs around her as though she did not even matter. She had let that dominate her decisions until she had backed herself into a corner. She had come back here to bust out of that corner and that old way of thinking. She might as well start now. "*My* house, Mike."

"Jo, let's be reasonable about this."

"Reasonable? You want reason when you're the one holding an open house for a property that isn't even yours to sell for potential buyers that don't even seem to exist?"

"Well, now, a little dose of reality here, Jo. You

did go off and leave the place in a pretty rough state."

Actually the place had left her in a pretty rough state.

"If you've really come here to see about unfinished business, maybe you should start by putting the finishing touches on that house."

She started to protest then caught herself. All this time she had fretted and stewed about all the money she still owed, but she hadn't given much thought to the money she already had invested—or the money she might recoup if she actually could sell that place. Maybe Mike had done her a favor by allowing the Brittneys to practice holding open houses with her property. The marketing part was done, all she had to do was . . . everything else.

"Maybe I'd better get over there as soon as possible. I have a whole lot of work to do before Sunday afternoon."

"That's the spirit." He gave her a friendly punch in the arm. "When life gives you lemons, make hay while the sun shines."

He got her to laugh, which she knew was his goal all along. Jo always went all gushy for a guy who made her laugh. The image of Travis flashed through her mind, all sun-kissed and . . . kissable.

She wondered what he was doing right now and if he missed her. Probably not. He was a busy man.

"Anyway, like you said, lot of work to do before Sunday." Mike's voice intruded on her thoughts. "There's a term for it. C'mon, you know. Use the day? It's in the Bible."

"Use the day? In the Bible?"

Mike had never shown any interest in her faith before and now he'd brought it up a couple of times. While she wanted to ask him about that, her mind had already rushed ahead trying to piece together what he meant by "use the day." "I think the verse you're thinking of is—"

"Carpe diem."

"Mike, that's not in the Bible."

"Seize the day!" He appeared so proud of himself. Too proud to let a little thing like being wrong deter him.

"That's Latin."

"Yeah, yeah. Like the Bible."

"No. Latin like . . ." Jo jerked her head up. If she had been in a comic strip, a lightbulb would have appeared over her head. "Like something else you liked to quote whenever I questioned your methods of selling house. Caveat emptor."

"Caveat? Naw." He tugged on her elbow to direct her into his spacious office. "If I said that, I'm sure I meant it as a joke, Jo."

"It's not an expression intended as a joke, Mike. It's intended as a warning." She reluctantly went along with his gentle urging to move into a private space.

How could she have worked for this man? How could she have gone into deal after deal with him, buying and reselling houses? How could she have had a crush on a man like Mike, then think a man like Travis could love her?

He shut the office door. "It's intended as a reminder, Jo. That each man—or woman—is responsible for his or her own choices."

She froze, unable to argue with that assessment.

"You think I'm too harsh?" he asked.

"No." She turned to face him. "I think I should have listened to your . . . *reminder* before I stretched my finances to the limit on my last house."

"Jo . . . how can I help?"

"What?"

He moved to his desk, pulled open a drawer and took out his company checkbook. "How 'bout I make this month's mortgage payment?"

The moment the offer left his lips Jo felt lighter. The tightness in her chest eased. She dropped into the chair opposite the desk and sighed. It wasn't a long-term solution but it would buy her enough time and reduce her stress enough to allow her to do as Travis had advised—to take responsibility for her own actions.

"You . . . you'd do that?"

Not Kate, not her mother, not even Travis had

offered Jo anything so concrete, so pragmatic so . . . helpful.

She looked up at the man in the white shirt and red tie sitting across from her with a black-and-gold pen poised over a blank check.

"But why, Mike?"

"Because I missed you?" he asked, a little too smoothly.

A few months ago that would have been enough for Jo. Today she shook her head. "You've watched me struggle with this house through nightmarish renovations, plummeting market values and personal crisis. Until this moment, you never offered to help before. Why now?"

He folded his hands on the open checkbook and looked her right in the eyes. "Because you always seemed to have a handle on everything, Jo. You made everything look so effortless, so . . ."

"Perfect," she whispered.

"Yeah. Perfect."

She clenched her teeth. She had spent so much of her life striving for just that. To do all the right things. To look just the right way. To be somebody worthy of being loved.

"Jo, until this very moment, as you put it, I never worried about you. I never thought I had to, you know, give you a second thought."

"Nobody does." Except . . . maybe . . . Travis.

"I never did because I always had so much

confidence in you. I always knew you'd be all right because . . . you're *you*."

Her whole life this was what she had wanted. For someone to see her and trust her. She had never imagined it would come from such an unlikely source.

"Thank you, Mike. You don't know what that means to me," she said softly. "If you can help with that payment, I'll put all my energy into getting that house sold. You won't be disappointed in me."

"I know I won't, Jo. I *know* I won't."

Chapter Seventeen

Kate flipped up the collar of her crisp pink-and-blue print shirt then ruffled her hand through her shaggy bangs to give them a carefree tousled look. She stepped back to check out her image in the full-length mirror inside the door of the closet under the stairs. She pursed her lips, frowned then smoothed down both her collar and her thick, sun-streaked brown hair.

"Goodness, child, you act as nervous as a teenager going out on her first babysitting job." Dodie settled into the plaid couch in the front room of the cottage and propped her stockinged feet up on the beat-up old coffee table. "Want Mama to sit by the phone in case you need to call for backup?"

Dodie was just having a little fun, of course. Still, it did give Kate some measure of comfort knowing that while Jo was in Atlanta, Moxie was working at the Bait Shack and Gentry and Pera were in Miami, there would be a trusted voice of experience nearby she could call on if she got overwhelmed. Not overwhelmed by caring for Fabbie, but by her own feelings for Vince.

Vince. Just standing here trying to decide what

to wear to spend the evening with him reduced her to a tangle of twitchy nerves and iffy emotions. She fussed with her collar again, frustrated by the way it seemed to mimic her erratic emotions. Up. Down. Out of control.

She heaved a sigh and went back to working with the stiff fabric. "I *so* want this to go well, Mom. It will be the first time Vince and I have done anything even remotely domestic since the days when Gentry was a kid and we took him on outings."

"You'll do fine. Now scoot."

"If only I knew—"

"Uh-uh! No, ma'am. No 'if onlys' allowed in this household!" Dodie held one finger up to cut Kate off sternly. "Nobody ever built a solid bond or a solid future on 'if only.' You want to nurture a relationship with Vince Merchant, those are two words you have to strike from your vocabulary right now, Scat-Kat Katie."

Kate cringed. She snapped her collar down and jerked it into place, muttering, "I'll strike 'if only' from my vocabulary if you'll strike 'Scat-Kat' from yours."

"Done."

Kate took her eyes off the image of her flustered reaction to face her mom, sitting on the ugly plaid couch surrounded by decades-old decor as if she was the queen of all she surveyed. Which she was.

Kate managed a tentative smile. "Scat-Kat Kate? Gone? Never to be heard from your lips again?"

Her mother made the classic "tick-a-lock" motion, pretended to turn a key to seal her lips.

"Really?"

"Really." She raised her hand as though pinching that invisible lip key between her thumb and fingers and then proceeded to pantomime tossing it over her shoulder. To her credit, she did not even pretend to look where it landed.

Kate made note of that because, well, Cromwell women did not just say what they meant, they meant a lot of stuff they did not say. They had a long history of taking some things too literally, taking some things too silently, and taking far too many things far too personally. If Dodie had just once glanced over her shoulder, even in jest, Kate would have taken that as a sign she planned to get that nonexistent key back just in case she ever wanted to take the horrid nickname out of the vault again.

"You just plan to stop saying it?"

"Better than a mere plan, I *promise* to stop saying it."

There it was. One of those said and unsaid deals, one of those things to be taken literally and meant personally. A plan? Everyone knew that was just a good intention which, as the saying went, "often goes astray." But a promise?

A promise from a mother to a daughter. From one longtime hurting and guardedly healing heart to another. From Dodie to Kate. Now *that* was a commitment.

"Oh, Mom." Kate went to the couch and wound her arms around her mother's shoulders. She laid her cheek on top of her mom's cotton candy–stiff but pliable bubble of pale hair. She drew in the smell of perfume barely masking the crisp scent of the astringent hand wash they were required to use at the hospital when visiting Billy J.

Dodie rested her warm cheek on Kate's forearm for a moment then gave her oldest daughter's hand a pat. "Now off with you. Vince is waiting."

She said it like "your future is waiting."

Kate kissed her mother's cheek then straightened and took a few hobbling steps back to the mirror. She gave herself one final glance, sighed, then headed for the door.

She had finally closed the cover on the Scat-Kat Katie chapter of her life. Time to move on and see what happened next. Her answers, or the beginnings of answers, lay just across the street.

Her pulse fluttered. She hurried for the door as fast as her cast and cane would let her, her damp palm gripped so tightly against the cold, brass cat's head topper that squeaked every time she pushed off to take another step.

Thump. Clunk. Squeak.
Thump. Clunk. Squeak.

189

Somehow she had thought the sound of rushing off to greet her future would have more dignity.

"Have a lovely time. Remember who you are."

Remember who you are.

It was Dodie's way of saying "mind your manners," "do your family proud," "be God's hands on earth." It meant she should comport herself like a Christian. And a doctor. And a lady. A potentially high-profile member of a small close-knit community Christian lady doctor.

Dodie had used the old Southern admonition on Kate many, many times before. She did not think Dodie ever had to use it on Jo, who always seemed to know exactly who she was and where she was going. Not like Kate. Not like good ol' Scat-Kat Katie.

She turned slowly to say good-night and instead heard herself asking, "Why?"

"Because I raised you to be somebody!" Dodie shot back, clearly more than a little surprised to find herself having to justify what seemed to her just common sense.

"It doesn't matter who you raised me to be, the persona I became, at least for a good deal of my life, was Scat-Kat Katie. You acknowledged that. Rubbed my nose in it a little more than I thought you should, in fact. Why abandon it now and so readily?"

"My gift to you." Dodie held both hands out, palms up, the way a person might hold a bird

190

with a newly mended wing about to set it free. "My way of letting you know how proud I am of the woman you've become, a woman who has stopped running away from life and started to embrace it."

"Oh, Mom." Kate made a step toward her mother. All the years they had spent torn to pieces inside and trying to look whole on the outside, all the ways they had tried to patch the two realities together, all the time they had lost looking for Molly Christina and often seeing right past each other came rushing back to Kate. All that time she had blamed herself for not being a better sister and saving her kidnapped sister, maybe she should have been thinking about how she could have been a better daughter to her brokenhearted mother. "Mom, I know I haven't always . . . I just want you to know . . . If I had it all to do again, I'd . . ."

Dodie laughed in a peculiarly maternal way. Her lips hardly moved beyond a faint smile but her eyes shone with humor and love. "I know, sweetie."

"If only . . ."

"Hey! None of that!" Dodie's hand flew up in the universal *stop right there* sign.

"I thought that just applied to me and Vince," Kate said, though not very convincingly.

Dodie shook her head. She wasn't buying that.

Kate smiled ruefully at her own slipup. She,

who had worried her mother might try to eyeball an imaginary key to her lips, had been the first of the pair of them to revert back to the old habit she had agreed to quit.

"Okay, but given our circumstances, it may be a lot harder for me to stop with the 'if onlys' than for you to drop that accursed nickname."

"Ahh." Dodie blinked a few times as though processing that information, then took a quick breath and opened her mouth.

"And, no, you may not substitute Blank Blank Katie for . . . that other name."

"Oh." Her shoulders slumped but only for a second before she perked up. "Right. You're absolutely right. I called you on a mere variation of if only. I shouldn't expect leniency on a masked version of what I promised to stop calling you."

Kate smiled and nodded. She turned and had just reached for the doorknob again when—

"It's going to be very difficult, you know."

Kate turned just her head. "To stop calling me that?"

"To keep yourself from going back to the oddly aching comfort of those words." Dodie gazed off toward the closet under the stairs.

It was in that closet where they had found the photos that had helped Moxie identify herself to them. They had been packed away there all these years, with the matching photo of Dodie and the missing baby hanging right on the wall of the Bait Shack Buffet. Summer after summer they had come here. Season after season Dodie had searched for her ex-husband and missing child, always sending back a reminder of each place she had looked to be placed in a memory garden just beside the back deck. So many summers. So many souvenirs. And Molly Christina had grown up right here where they could have found her so easily.

"If only," Dodie murmured again before she gave her head a shake and sat up straight, her whole demeanor charged with a kind of purposeful energy. "Don't surrender to it. Take it from a woman whose whole life could have been reduced to those two words."

Kate tensed. The average outsider looking at their recently reunited family might think all those old issues would have evaporated. But a lifetime of wondering, of guilt, of sadness wasn't so easily shaken.

They all felt it. The residue of their past clung to every interaction. It colored the way they talked, the way they saw themselves and each other in much the same way the sense of emptiness and grief over having lost Molly Christina as a baby had. It was the kind of life experience that shaped and defined them as people and as a family.

"If only I had done this or known that, if only it had been different. You will never find contentment down that road, Katie. You will never make peace with the way things *are*. What might have been will always cut a chasm between you and moving forward."

Kate nodded.

"You have to turn away from that temptation, Katie. Let it go. When you came to terms with having walked away from Vince and Gentry all those years ago, you said the verse from First Corinthians had guided you."

" 'When I was a child I thought like a child . . .' "

"The person you were, the one you hold responsible for Molly Christina's fate, the one who ran away from happiness, was a child compared to who you are today. Let that child go, Kate."

"Thank you, Mom," Kate whispered through a shimmer of unshed tears.

Though she had not said it outright, Kate heard in her mother's words the forgiveness Kate had so long withheld from herself. From this moment on she would no longer worry that Dodie blamed Katie for not telling anyone sooner that her father had been in the house just before Molly Christina went missing.

Dodie sniffled, then gave her daughter a wave and said, "Enough of that, now! Vince is waiting. Your whole new life is waiting!" She cleared her throat. "Go and claim it."

Kate blew her mother a kiss and headed out the door.

Chapter Eighteen

"No!" The dark-haired toddler craned her neck to turn her head away from the dollop of strained carrots that her grandfather offered her. Every muscle in her compact body stiffened. She spread her fingers and even her toes as her arms and legs flailed.

"C'mon, Fabbie." Vince followed the dodging and weaving of her head with the spoon. "Just one bite."

"Careful what you ask for there, Vince." Kate bent down, kid level. "From the look in her eyes, I think she might just bite you."

"If she doesn't, her mom might when she gets back." Vince dropped the plastic spoon onto the food-caked tray of the child's high chair. "I don't think this child has actually swallowed more than a mouthful this whole evening."

She gave the man a gentle nudge to get him to relinquish his seat directly in front of Fabbie. "Here, let me try."

"Kate, I've been doing this since the kid went on solid foods." His resistance shone through in everything from his posture to the tone of his voice but he rose from the chair, his arm extended to welcome her graciously to the task. "What makes you think you can do a better job with it?"

Kate tensed. "There were three things wrong with what you just said. Shall I enumerate them?"

He shook his head, smiled a big goofy grin at her and held out the spoon.

Kate took it, snatched it away, really, then softened toward him and laughed.

Vince laughed, too.

It felt good to share this evening with him, and yet it didn't entirely take the sting out of his reminder that she remained an interloper in his family.

"I am a doctor, you know," she couldn't help throwing out as she moved past him toward the uncooperative baby seated in the bright, cheery kitchen.

"You're a podiatrist, Kate. That's like being a specialist in the opposite end of the baby that's giving me fits. Now if she had issues squishing strained carrot between her toes . . ."

He reached out and lifted up one fat, pink baby foot spotted with globs of green and orange. "Then I could see where your expertise would come in handy."

"My expertise also includes emergency-room medicine." She swatted his hand away from Fabbie's ankle. She seated herself in front of the baby and bent her nose just inches from Fabbie's face, as though they were longtime girlfriends commiserating about the difficulties of dealing with the men in their lives.

Fabbie scooted closer, too, her small hands gripping the edge of the tray.

"Tell your grandfather that I've quieted plenty of little ones in my life." Kate lowered her voice in a tone of shared confidences. Then sputtered her lips, made a face and stuck her tongue out of the side of her mouth.

Fabbie giggled.

This wasn't so hard. Kate pushed the bowl of baby food back in front of the child. "You just have to get their attention. Don't you, Fabbie? Grown-ups aren't the only ones who enjoy a little dinner theater. Are they?"

Fabbie clapped.

Kate pulled her shoulders up. "You have a long record of approaching child care by trying to control the outcome of every encounter, Vince. You never learned to pick your battles."

Fabbie shoved the bowl across the tray toward Kate.

Kate met the child's determined gaze with one of her own in which she tried to telegraph the message, *I'm making a point here, kid, work with me.*

Another shove.

The bowl wobbled.

Vince snickered but said nothing.

Kate plastered the sweetest smile she could muster on her face and cooed to the baby. "Okay. So you want the bowl at the edge of the tray. No problem."

Kate very calmly wriggled her chair over to clear herself from any potential drop zone for falling food or bowls. She then turned and looked at Vince. She could do this. She did not have to have been involved in this child's life every day up until this point to make a connection with her. She could be a part of this family if he would only ask her to.

"Sometimes you have to roll with the punches," she told him, talking about far more than just poking food into an uncooperative child. "You start where you are and work with what you've been given."

She held up the spoon.

He watched her intently.

So intently she could not tear her gaze from his, or hide the double meaning in her words as she said, "It's not so hard, really. You'd be surprised what people can do when they just—"

Splat!

A tiny handful of baby food hit Kate across her cheek and nose.

For a moment, silence practically crackled in the air.

Then Vince burst out laughing.

Kate sat there for several seconds more before

198

she got over the shock enough to make a sound. To Kate's surprise, the sound she made was a warm, heartfelt peal of giggles.

"I really don't know that much about babies. I just thought . . ." She looked at the wriggling child then at him.

She swept her gaze across the small kitchen and into the nearby front room, the small space that both defined and disclosed almost nothing about Vince. She looked at the school photos of Gentry as a child hanging on the wall and the snapshots of Fabbie stuck to the fridge. In a matter of seconds she took in the highlights of what Vince found important in life. She tried not to think too much about the fact that there was nothing of her to be found. She was the one sitting here helping him care for his grandchild after all.

He loved her.

She loved him.

"I thought—how hard can this be?" she confessed.

Vince opened his mouth to say something, cocked his head then frowned. "We're not just talking about feeding Fabbie now, are we?"

Kate took one last look around, put the spoon aside and stood. "No, we're not."

"Yeah. I thought so." Vince grabbed a dish towel and came to her. "You had that look."

"What look?" Kate reached out to take the towel from him.

He yanked it away. "Hold still."

She wanted to protest that she could take care of herself. Then he placed his large hand gently along the side of her neck.

As the warmth from his palm sank slowly into her tight muscles, Kate shut her eyes and sighed.

The nubby fabric of the cloth moved in circles over her skin as he dabbed off the goop on her face. After a moment, he stepped back to inspect his handiwork.

"Better?" she asked, lifting her tentative gaze to his.

"Just a smudge more right . . ." He placed his thumb at the center of her lower lip.

His touch made her shiver.

"There. That's the last of it."

"Are you sure?" she asked coyly.

"Maybe I should take a closer look." He leaned in.

Whap. Splat. Clunk.

This time the runny mix of green and orange mush came at them spoon and all. Fabbie didn't have the oomph to throw the thing hard enough to reach their faces but hit Vince's knuckles just as he was raising his hand to run his fingers through Kate's hair. Which caused him to spread baby food from her temple to the back of her head.

"Oh, Kate. I'm sorry."

"Yuck!" She thought she could simply brush the mess away but found herself inadvertently rubbing it deeper in. She withdrew her hand and stared at her gooey fingers. "When you said Fabbie would be our chaperone I never dreamed she'd take the role so seriously."

"She has done a great job of keeping us apart so far," he admitted.

"So many things have tried to keep us apart so far, Vince, Fabbie is going to have to come up with something a whole lot better than flinging a little food."

"I know a way to foil her scheme." Vince lifted the baby from her seat. "We'll see if a little time in a warm bathtub changes your tune."

"Actually it's not her tune that needs changing." Kate put her finger under her nose.

Fabbie kicked both legs like a jumping frog and squealed.

Vince kept his grip on the child even as he held her at arm's length. "So I guess this is out of your area of expertise, *Dr.* Cromwell?"

He was actually going to let her help! Sure, with the messiest and *stinkiest* duty of the evening. Not the kind of job you asked an outsider to do. She reached out. "Give me that baby."

Half an hour later everything was back to normal—the high chair, Fabbie, Kate's hair and . . .

Kate looked up from the crib where she had

just put the sleepy child to see Vince staring at her.

"What? Did I get soap all over my clothes? Powder on my cheek?" She swiped her palm down the side of her head. "Is there still strained carrot in my hair?"

"You're beautiful."

She relaxed and let her gaze dip to the floor, shy but just a bit flirtatious. "Yes, I've heard the almost-forty, wet-haired, foot-in-cast look is all the rage on the Paris runways this year."

"If it isn't, it should be." He extended his hand to lead her out of the room. "But I wasn't talking about the way you look."

"Oh?"

"I mean, you look good. You look—" he pulled her not just into the hallway but into his arms then gazed down into her eyes "—real good."

"Thank you, Vince."

"When I called you beautiful, I was trying to tell you that you . . . you're . . ."

"Yes?"

He touched her cheek. "You're beautiful."

"So you said. Twice." Not that she minded hearing it repeated. "And?"

Fabbie let out a low, drawn-out mewl.

Kate froze.

Vince made a move to go for the baby.

She nabbed his arm and held him in place.

When Fabbie cried out again, she tiptoed into

Gentry's old room and stole a peek into the crib.

"Shh." She stroked back the baby's dark, slightly damp hair. "Go to sleep, sweetie. You need to gather your strength to throw oatmeal at Grandpa in the morning."

"Hey! Don't give her ideas!"

More fussing.

Kate patted the baby's back. "We beautiful girls have to stick together."

As if agreeing with Kate's assessment, Fabbie let out a hearty burp.

Vince let out a laugh.

"Hey, beauty is as beauty burps." She dropped a kiss on the drowsy baby's head then made her way back to the hallway.

He followed her with his eyes, making her feel self-conscious.

"Anyway, I'm not beautiful. That's Jo. I'm more the clean-cut wholesome girl-next-door type of attractive."

"You were always pretty, Kate." His hand fit around the nape of her neck. He tipped his head to one side, his eyes dark. "But now, knowing what you've done with your life, seeing how you take care of people, the way you care about me? Pretty just doesn't do you justice."

"I'm not doing anything special," she whispered.

"But what you are doing looks good on you," he murmured. "You look good with a baby, Kate."

His words virtually stole her breath away. Still, she managed to get out a very soft, "Do I?"

"Yeah. Very good." He tucked a strand of hair behind her ear then let his fingertips trace the path from her earlobe down her jaw. "Makes a guy wonder."

She stiffened. "Makes a guy wonder what?"

He crooked his finger beneath her chin and tipped it so that she could only gaze up into his sincere, searching eyes as he said, "Not 'what' but 'what if.' "

"Hold it right there." Her stiffness turned to downright rigidity. She pulled away from his touch and held her hand up between them. "I just made a promise not to surrender to the temptation of the words *if only.*"

"I didn't say 'if only.' " He placed both of his large hands on her tightly raised shoulders and lowered his face until the entire world seemed to narrow to the two of them. "I said 'what if.' Big difference."

"There is?" she murmured, mesmerized by the possibility.

" 'If only' speaks of regret."

If only she had been a better Christian and turned to God and prayer for answers instead of running from hard realities. If only she had been a braver sister and spoken up when Molly Christina disappeared or paid more attention when they were in Santa Sofia and found the

204

connection sooner. If only she had been a bolder woman, willing to stand and fight for what she wanted.

"Regrets," she repeated softly. "Yeah. I see that."

"Whereas 'what if' dreams about possibilities."

What if she started trying to do all that now —living her faith, bonding with her sisters, standing and fighting for what she wanted?

Kate smiled. "I like that distinction."

"Good."

She put her hands on his chest. "So go with it."

"Go with . . . what?"

"Not 'what' but 'what if.' You said I looked good with a baby and it made a guy wonder." *You were just about to propose,* she wanted to tell him. Instead she just prodded, "What if?"

"Oh, yeah. Seeing you in my home like this, knowing it's a temporary thing this weekend, got me thinking."

"What if," she prodded yet again.

He nodded, squared his shoulders and came out with it, sort of. "What if you had a chance to do the caring for me and mine, doing baby duty and more, on a . . . let's call it a nontemporary basis."

Was *that* a proposal at last?

Kate didn't even know. A chance? Caring for him? Baby duty?

Wait. Had he said *baby?*

205

She could not concentrate on the question of marriage with this new twist stirring in her being. A baby. With Vince.

If she had not broken their engagement all those years ago, she would have expected that at some point she and Vince would have been . . . well, expecting. But now? With him as a grandfather and her thirty-nine?

It was not impossible but it did seem an unlikely dream. *"What if" dares to dream.*

Dare to dream, Kate. Stay and fight for that dream . . . on a nontemporary basis. That's what he was asking her.

"Yes," she said, before she overthought it and scared herself off.

She'd lived her life running away, afraid she'd make another mistake she could not undo. Now the man she loved stood before her asking her to commit to that very thing—to marriage and motherhood, two things that if Kate undertook, she could never run out on.

"Yes," she said again as she wrapped her arms around the man and laid her cheek on his chest.

"Yes?"

"Yes!" She said it louder this time then went up on tiptoe and kissed him to back it up.

"Kate, that's great." He brushed her hair back then kissed her briefly.

It was great. But was that all he was going to say about it? All he intended to do?

No bended knee? No whoop of joy? No grabbing her up and twirling her around?

Okay, that last one probably never would have occurred to him, given her big old cast and banged-up tootsie. Still, for her having accepted his proposal after their having loved and lost and loved one another over all these years, for her having said she would have his babies and take care of him and not run off? Kate felt a twinge of disappointment that his reaction wasn't bigger.

He put his hands on either side of her face and smiled. "So let's get this straight. If Gentry and Pera do move to Miami, you'll move, too, to give us a shot at being a family."

"Move?" She hadn't thought about moving. "Well, I guess . . . if that's where you go, I suppose I'd have to . . ."

"Are you having second thoughts?"

"It's just that I thought I'd found my home here in Santa Sofia. This is where I thought I'd grow old." *With you.* "It's where my family is all together, now, finally. It's where, you know, I thought we'd raise our family."

"Raise our *what?*" He stepped away from her.

"Don't act so shocked." She tried to laugh it off but the look of confusion tinged with a tiny bit of horror in his face made her feel anything but funny. "You're the one who brought up babies."

"I meant Fabbie." He pointed to the closed door of the room where the baby lay sleeping.

"Fabbie? But she's not *our* child, Vince."

"I know that. She's my grandchild, though. And I thought, you know, when I looked after her in the future, I'd want you around, too."

Nontemporarily. Meaning not on a temporary basis. Yet also, to a man who made such a clear distinction between "what if" and "if only," a very carefully selected term. Not temporary, but also clearly not permanent.

Kate stepped back again, putting more than enough space between them so that, even with his arm outstretched, his hand no longer rested on her upper arm. "Vince, just what *exactly* were you asking me to nontemporarily do?"

"I wasn't asking you to *do* anything, Kate. I just wondered if maybe, *if* it came down to it, if you'd consider—"

"That's too many 'ifs,' Vince." Another step back. Yes, she was literally as well as emotionally retreating. She had to. She had finally taken a stand. "I'm not talking dreams or regrets. I'm talking reality. Mine and yours, Vince. I'm talking the future I want to build for myself, for us if that's what you want."

"My future is pretty unsettled right now, Kate. What with my whole family possibly going to pick up and move to a new city."

Not your whole family, Vince. She wanted to

say it but if she did she'd never know if he really saw her as his family or if he simply acquiesced to smooth things out between them. "So you're saying?"

"I can't really say anything until I know what my family plans to do and can decide what's best for them."

"I see." She nodded and took another step back. "Well, then, I guess that doesn't leave me any choice but to go home."

"Kate, what's wrong? I don't understand."

"The fact that you don't understand is what's wrong, Vince." She turned at last and headed for the door.

"I'll see you tomorrow, though, right?" he called after her.

"You're staying in the house across the cul-de-sac from my home." The cottage on Dream Away Bay Court, her home? She'd said it and she'd meant it. "I promised I'd help take care of Fabbie. I'm not running out on my promises ever again, Vince. If you need me, you will see me tomorrow."

"And if I don't?"

Don't see me or don't need me? Kate didn't dare ask. She just slipped through the door with a silent wave and waited until she'd gotten all the way onto her own front porch before she broke down and began to sob her heart out.

Chapter Nineteen

Not since she'd discovered her now-infamous Cromwell connection had Moxie had an evening like this. A six-hour shift at the Bait Shack for which she would receive not one dime in pay, and what tips she'd earn, she'd share with some deserving member of the staff.

Before learning about her long-lost family?

This was how she spent pretty much every weekend evening for . . . too many years. Back then, she'd resigned herself to it and spent most of the time trying not to dwell on her situation. Tonight she reveled in it.

With the good news from the hospital that they wanted to release Billy J tomorrow, not because they were sick of him, as she had been telling people as a joke, but because he was well enough to come home, her worries had lightened. With Jo out of town, Kate spending time with Vince and Dodie resting up for the trip to get Billy J tomorrow, Moxie finally had an evening all to herself.

Well, not *all* to herself.

"I don't know that this really made any difference, Moxie." Hunt clunked an empty glass pitcher onto the counter at the drink station, which had originally been a bar in the days before Billy J made the place a family establishment.

He cocked his head and exhaled in a long stream, his way of telling her he'd had enough of waiting tables and interacting with pretty much everyone eating out in Santa Sofia tonight.

"The last customer is out, Moxie. The drawers are balanced, bank deposit in the safe, kitchen clean. Want me to lock the door and turn the sign on my way out?" The night manager had the experience and the authority to pretty much do anything except sell the place for less than market value, so the question she called out was merely a show of courtesy. And a very thinly disguised way of letting Moxie know the staff was leaving and she and Hunt had the place to themselves.

"Thanks!" Moxie gave a wave.

"Great working with ya!" Hunt waved, too, then turned to Moxie. "Who was that?"

"She ordered you around all night, and you never learned her name?"

"If I tried to learn the names of everyone who ordered me around tonight . . . well, why would I bother? It would be easier to just carry around the Santa Sofia phone book. That almost sums up the list."

She contemplated sticking out her lower lip

and giving him a sweet and sympathetic "poor baby" but thought better of it. Hunt Diamante was anything but a baby. He'd taken her suggestion to work here tonight like a man. She got the feeling he took everything like a man and gave back in kind.

So instead of talking down to him, even in an act of good-natured coddling, she decided to let him know he wasn't the only person who had busted his behind all night. "Welcome to my world."

"You do this often?"

Too often. That would sound as if she had no other life beyond these walls. No *social* life at least.

She didn't have, really. Even though she had dated Lionel for years she had still ended up here most weekends. Working when her dad needed her, sitting and yakking with Lionel and friends when he didn't.

Yet for all that time spent here, none of it had felt as productive as tonight. Productive and . . . exhilarating.

She looked across the tall counter at Hunt and suddenly she knew why. "It wasn't so bad, was it? Spending time with me here?"

"Naw." The sole of his athletic shoe squawked against the brass foot rail. "Not bad at all."

"Good." *Good.* What a perfect word to describe this guy. Good work ethic. Good heart. Good-looking.

She eased out a soft, dreamy sigh and gazed at him for so long that he finally waved his hand in front of her face.

"Hey? Drift off for a minute?"

"Oh! I . . ." She blinked, rapidly trying to come up with a clever remark to cover for her lapse in conversation.

You are so cute.

Do you like me?

Will you be my new boyfriend?

A list of geeky questions clicked through her mind. Happily none of them made it all the way to her mouth.

"Um, yes, good. Glad you enjoyed working here tonight. You'll see results at the *Sun Times* from it, too. You've made more inroads than you think."

"Inroads? By pouring an ocean of sweet tea? Sweet tea? Honestly?"

Moxie yanked the wayward pitcher he had collected down into a small sink filled with hot sudsy water. "You've heard the old saying that the way to a man's heart is through his stomach?"

Hunt narrowed his eyes. "Yeah, so?"

"Well, the way to Santa Sofia's heart is through . . ." She motioned with her hand, encouraging him to complete the sentence.

He hazarded a guess. "Through . . . a straw?"

"Service!" She popped a dish towel in his general direction. "A straw? The way to our town's heart is through a straw?"

"Big straw." He spread his hands wide. "You know, for drinking the sweet tea?"

She reached down and pulled the heavy pitcher up, setting it on the countertop with a solid *plunk* to dry. "You do not drink sweet tea through a straw."

"How do you drink it?"

"Um, let's see, you sip tea. You gulp it. And you . . . hmm." She went through the motions of drinking from her invisible glass again, trying to think of other words for the way locals consumed their favorite beverage. "You—"

"You shower in it?" He had come around the side of the drink station and almost fallen into a huge pillow of trash bag filled with nothing but disposable "go cups" that people had gotten to take with them when they went home, except most of them did not go home, but sat and visited with friends the whole night long. "That's what I'm guessing, judging from the number of these you go through around here. And that's not counting all the actual glasses I made the rounds filling every few minutes."

"Maybe they just liked the service," she teased.

"This is where I came into this conversation." He parked the dish sack on the counter to get a better grip.

Moxie slung a hand towel over her shoulder

and reached for the sack. "Here, you've done enough. I'll take care of—"

Her fingers curved around to gather the opening of the sack together just seconds before Hunt's hand closed over hers.

"Those," she mumbled to finish her directive just as she lifted her head and found herself instantly lost in Hunt's unwavering gaze.

She'd had her eyes on him all night. To make sure he didn't do his cause—or her daddy's customers—any harm, of course.

Still he didn't make a bad picture with the sleeves of his white dress shirt rolled up to expose his strong forearms and the pencil stuck behind his ear standing out against the bristle of his short dark hair. He'd hustled hard all evening long, making a big show of his exasperation but with his smile always just beneath the surface ready to break free.

And now here he stood, his fingers entwined with hers. "You really think working here one night will leave any kind of lingering impression?"

"It already has," she whispered.

"How do you know? You soliciting orders for ad space behind my back?"

"Ad space?" Moxie crinkled her nose, released the bag and took a step backward. "No. I can't promise . . . It's just that people like to deal with people they feel they know and—"

215

"That's what I thought." He made quick work of tying up the bag's top.

His broad shoulders sloped forward. He rubbed his hands over his face then looked out at the now-empty dining room of the Bait Shack.

He'd worked so hard tonight. Not just pouring tea but pouring on the charm, and not that false "salesman desperate for a sale" kind of charm, either. The real, intense, encompassing charm of a man doing what he did best—listening, learning. A true journalist who loved to find the story behind the story, not just the headline, not just the sound bite. He had talked to the people he met here tonight. Really talked. He had gotten people she had lived near, worked with, shared church pews and chugged sweet tea with for most of her life to share tidbits that she had never known about—everything from their most embarrassing Bait Shack moment to their most moving example of what life in Santa Sofia meant to them.

"Hey, it might not mean tons more ads right away, but it's a start."

"A start?" He shook his head. "You got a bank around here who lets a guy write a check 'on the start of a good impression'?"

Bank? Was money the problem?

"Oh! I almost forgot." She dived into the pocket of her apron and pulled out a wad of bills. "Here."

"What's this?"

"Your tips. You've earned them."

"No. Thank you, but no." He pushed the money toward her.

She pushed back. "Don't be so proud. You came here to learn more about people in Santa Sofia. Well, first lesson—we help each other out."

"I already got that from hearing their stories tonight, Moxie. I don't need this—"

"Lesson two." She held up two fingers. "Everybody has hard times. We're a has-been tourist town. There isn't anyone around who doesn't know what an empty pocket feels like."

"Hard times? Empty pockets?" He bowed his head, shook it, then met her gaze again, his eyes somber. "Moxie, you have no idea who I am, do you?"

"Hunt Diamante?" She curled her wad of tip money in close to her chest, adding softly, "New editor of the *Santa Sofia Sun Times*?"

"Not quite." He held his hands up, as though substantiating an invisible wall between them. "I'm *R*. Hunt Diamante. Reinhardt . . . Hunter . . . Diamante."

"Reinhardt? That's your first name?"

"And my mother's maiden name." He paused with such purpose that Moxie felt like his partner in a game of charades. His very dense partner. One who didn't have the slightest idea what his clues meant.

She stared at him and fought to make a conscious effort not to let her face squish up with concentration. Yes, even as she tried to piece together the mystery that was Reinhardt Hunter Diamante, she wanted to look her best doing it.

"Maybe you've heard of her family? Reinhardt? Reinhardt *Media?*"

"Reinhardt Media Enterprises?"

"It's a big media conglomerate . . . Very powerful. Very influential. Very—"

"Bad news . . ."

Tidbits of the conversation the family had had on the day they had gathered to read the botched article sprang to Moxie's mind. "That's you?"

"That's my family."

"Wow. Your family runs a big media conglomerate and you're a newspaper editor?" She leaned an elbow on the drink station and rested her chin in her hand. "I guess if you think about it, that does sort of make sense."

"No, Moxie, it doesn't make sense at all." He reached for her upraised hand and slid it gently away from her head, using it to lead her around the trash bag until she stood face-to-face with him. When he spoke to her again, he did so quietly and with only a few inches separating them. "I'm *not* a newspaper editor. I work for my family."

"But you're listed as the editor. That's not a lie, is it?"

"Well, no. Not a lie. I can . . . I have a degree in journalism. In fact I love the newspaper business, even though some people think its days are numbered."

"I can see how you'd be good at it," she said.

"That's hardly the consensus after the story I did on your reunion with your mother and sisters."

"You didn't let me finish," she went on. "I can see how you'd be good at it, *if* you'd let yourself care enough to do what you're clearly capable of."

"Thanks."

"I saw that in the way you worked tonight. You really showed an interest in people. And you didn't mind getting your hands dirty." She kicked at the trash bag he had not minded handling.

"I worked my way up from sales to obituaries to hard news at one of my family's larger papers. I've put in the hours and have the know-how. I just . . ." He rubbed his hand back over his closely cropped hair. "This is how it is —I blow into town when we've bought a new newspaper. I run them long enough to see if they can turn a profit and if not . . ."

He left the rest to her imagination. Only it didn't take any imagination at all.

"You've come to close the *Sun Times*?"

"Not if it . . ." He spread his hands and looked around. Finally, nodded his head. "Yeah, that's pretty much what's going to happen."

"Then what happens to you?"

"Me? Well, then, I guess *I* move on and do it all over again."

"You guess? It's not set in stone?"

"Stone? No. I . . ." More head rubbing. "I guess I can do pretty much whatever I want."

"You can do whatever you want and your family won't freak out on you?"

He gave her a cool, lopsided grin at that. "Reinhardts never *freak out,* Moxie."

She took all that in. Freedom *and* family. Plus, no freak-outs. "You have the greatest job I have ever heard of."

"Huh?"

"Think about it. You work for your family but you don't have to work *with* your family. You get to travel, meet lots of new people."

He hung his head. "Sometimes I have to close down local landmarks."

She put her hand on his. The downside of his work had certainly taken its toll. This, however, was something she understood. "But it's not your job to close them. It's your job to turn them around. Sometimes you do that, right? Save them?"

"Hmm. Yeah, I guess sometimes I do."

"See, it's like that in my business, too."

He looked around them.

"Not the Bait Shack. I own my own property management company, remember?"

"Oh, yeah. It's just I've never seen you in action, that's all."

She laughed. "Yeah, I know it sounds pretty dull to a guy in your line of work, with your background and all, but in the end it's not so different."

"Really?"

"That's right. You get to hear a lot of really fascinating stories then have to ferret out the truth about them and the people telling them."

"I'll bet."

"You try to make things work. You want people to have a home, not to lose their investment. Sometimes that's not to be."

"Yeah." He looked at his shoes.

"But when you can make that happen? When your hard work can turn things around for others?"

"The way to their heart is through service?" he offered.

"Yep."

"The *Sun Times* exists to serve the community?" He referenced their earlier conversation about the purpose of a local newspaper. "So if I serve the community, the town will take me into their hearts and—"

"We'll save the *Sun Times*."

"Moxie, I can't promise that."

"Oh." She took a step, remembered the trash bag, turned, picked it up then faced him, her smile returning to her face. "Well, still you have

221

another chance somewhere else and you don't have your family crowding in on you."

"There is that." He took the bag from her.

She nudged him. "Aren't you going to give me some kind of lecture about how much you wish your family cared about you as much as mine cares about me and how they only do what they do because they love me and want the best for me?"

"Why? The very fact that you're saying that to me means you already know it."

She led the way to the back of the Bait Shack, where they could dump the trash on their way to their cars. "You are a keen observer of human nature, Hunt."

"Naw, just of *certain* humans."

She whipped her head around to catch him smiling.

"The ones I can't keep my eyes off, the ones I want to know more about."

She smiled, too, only she didn't let him see it. Then she headed for the door, grateful for the dim lighting to hide the flustered blush on her cheeks. "I think you're going to do your best to save the *Times*. You really are a nice guy, after all."

"Ha!" He stepped out of the back door and pitched the trash bag into the Dumpster.

Moxie leaned against the fender of her truck. "Well, you did get out of your car the first day we met to try to help me. That was awfully nice."

He came up beside her and looked down into her face, an overly exaggerated scowl on his face. "You were in my way."

Am I in your way now? She wanted to ask it, wanted to know both why he had stopped to stand so close to her and if there was any chance that her being in Santa Sofia might keep him here no matter what happened at the *Times*. Instead of all that, she simply asked, "You really going to leave in a few months?"

"Why do you want to know?" he asked softly.

"I just wonder if it's worth it." Testing boundaries. She hadn't really believed she had it in her, yet here she was, not just testing, but actually pushing at them.

"Wonder if *what's* worth it? Saving the *Sun Times*?"

"No."

"What, then?" He inched just a little closer.

She rolled her eyes. He sure wasn't making this easy. "I'm going to use this tip money to go toward paying for that ad I promised to run." Every last word dripped with sarcasm. Maybe he'd pick up on that.

"Then you have your answer. It's not worth it. You don't have to run that ad."

The sarcasm fell away. She raised her chin and gazed up into his eyes. "But I want to."

"Why? I've seen the business this place does.

You don't need to spend money on an ad to keep people coming through the doors."

She didn't know if he was being dense or a gentleman or if he was genuinely trying to look out for her by releasing her from a bad business move. "What if I only care about whether one person keeps coming through the door?"

"One? Lot of trouble to go to for one person. Doesn't seem like good business to me."

"Lesson three." She held up three fingers.

"Let me guess. What's good for business is not always good, or right. Sometimes serving others is more important than showing a profit. True?"

"True but that wasn't what I was going to say." Now she moved close. Not in a predatory way but just so that if her nerve failed her, she could still make herself heard.

"What were you going to say?"

"Lesson three. Quit being so dense. *You* are the person I want to keep coming through the doors."

"Then don't bother with that ad. I can't be bought. I told you that."

He stepped in and put his hand under her chin, tipping her head back. "You can challenge me, you can make me crazy, that only makes me more determined."

"More determined to do what?" she asked, keenly aware that every word seemed to put her mouth in position to be kissed.

224

"To do the right thing." He kissed her, but only lightly, then stepped away. "That's all I can promise you, Moxie. I'll do right by the town, the paper, and, if you really want me to keep coming through the door, by you."

"Oh, Hunt."

"But I can't promise you—"

She put her hand over his lips. "Let's not talk about what we can't promise tonight. You do your best. I'll do mine. We'll leave the outcome to the Lord."

Chapter Twenty

Leave it with the Lord.

What a simple plan. A perfect plan. Sometimes a nearly impossible plan.

Moxie did not think she had gotten more than a couple of hours' sleep after saying good-night to Hunt and before having to get up to go over to the Cromwell cottage to pick up Kate and Dodie. In those hours of nonsleep she had gone over the events of the evening again and again. She had run through various projections of what all could go wrong the next morning. When not doing either of those, she had found her mind wandering to thoughts about what it meant to have a family, to be a part of a family and maybe . . . someday . . . to *start* a family.

That had led her mind to thoughts of Hunt. Then of babies. Then of what she and Hunt's baby might look like. Then of how little she knew of his background . . . and of how little she knew of her *own* background.

Which brought her back to the hard realities of her feelings about the Cromwells, what had happened and what would happen next.

She just couldn't seem to work through her feelings.

She liked the Cromwells. On some level that she had yet to explore, she believed she loved them. Given time—and space—that love would surely grow. As she had admitted to Hunt last night, she recognized what a blessing it was to have found them. And yet there was something about them she could not get past.

Something about Dodie, most of all.

Every time she had to spend time around Dodie, Moxie went on the defensive. She couldn't help it. She knew how much the woman wanted to forge a bond, to reconnect, to simply love Moxie and be loved in return. To hear Moxie, after all these years, call her Mom.

Moxie could not do that.

It made her feel awful. Miserable. Like a rotten daughter.

Leaving it with the Lord?

It seemed the only thing Moxie hadn't tried.

Her restless mind, unsettled heart and sleep-deprived body did not leave her in the cheeriest of moods the next morning.

"Y'all did not have to come along to pick up my dad this morning." Moxie slid behind the wheel of Dodie's car, and slammed the door. She'd been looking forward to, and dreading this, all week.

Now she had to add this to the emotional Ping-Pong match going on in her head.

Dad's coming home.

Good!

Dad's going to need a lot of looking after and her life was crowded enough already.

Bad!

He wasn't in danger anymore.

Good!

She wasn't going to have a moment of peace, much less time to explore a relationship with Hunt and help save the newspaper.

Bad!

Moxie had hoped to work through this without the distraction of Dodie and Kate acting as cheering section, coach and critic over every point she tried to grapple with.

"We don't mind, dear." Dodie dropped into the passenger seat then clicked the seat belt decisively into place.

But she never felt she got a moment away from them, or from anticipating when they would expect something of her again.

Kate squirmed in the backseat. When she got herself and her cast comfortably situated, she said, "That's what families do. When their loved ones need something, families come through."

"Come through, not *come along*. They are not the same thing." It had popped into her head and right out of her mouth.

Let the games begin, she thought, already feeling a dull headache building as the metaphorical little ball she had chosen to represent all her issues began pinging around her brain, never seeming to miss a chance to skip and pop over her very last nerve.

"Molly Christina!"

"I'm sorry. It's not that I don't appreciate you lending me the car, Dodie." Moxie pulled out of the drive. "I do. It's just . . ."

"Late night at the Bait Shack?" Dodie folded her hands in her lap. She kept her eyes forward but the hint of a catlike smile playing on her lips told Moxie her birth mother knew how to play the game, and play to win.

"How did you know about me and Hunt?" Moxie shot back.

"She didn't until you said that!" Kate might as well have said, "One point, Mom. Moxie, nothing," into a microphone in that faux whisper sports announcers sometimes use.

Moxie groaned. "I just assumed somebody who ate there last night said something."

"And you accuse *us* of closing in on you!" Kate laughed wryly. "Seems to me that by growing up in Santa Sofia as Billy J's daughter you've had a lifetime of training for life with an obnoxiously close family."

"So." Dodie shifted just enough in the seat to put herself at an angle to hear every word and catch every nuance of Moxie's tense expression. "What's this about you and Hunt?"

This car was definitely too small.

Kate stretched forward as far as she could in the backseat. "At the Bait Shack, you say? Until all hours?"

And getting smaller by the second.

Moxie glanced over her shoulder at her big sister and made a face. "I thought sisters were supposed to have each other's backs in situations like this."

"All's fair in love and war." Kate's eyes glittered, clearly enjoying Moxie's discomfort at having her love life, such as it was, offered up for speculation as the topic du jour.

"Girls, girls!" Dodie gave one sharp clap of her hands. "It's a sisterhood, not a competition."

"I'm beginning to think those two things are not as diametrically opposed as you make them out to be, Dodie." *All's fair in love and war?* Well, if it was war her sister wanted . . . "As for me and Hunt it was all out in the open. He pitched in serving at the Bait Shack to help improve his profile in the community. He and I are not at war, Kate, and we certainly haven't known one another long enough to be in love. Can you say the same about you and Vince?"

"For someone who says she doesn't get the whole 'intrusive family, sisterhood as a competition' dynamic, you sure are awfully crafty at it." Kate scowled, but beneath that scowl Moxie could see the kind of grudging admiration that she suspected belonged solely to the realm of siblings.

She liked it. Liked it even more when the light of scrutiny shifted away from her and Hunt and onto the ongoing travails of Kate and Vince and the stage of waiting for him to pop the question.

Kate didn't give a definitive answer, either. However, she took the rest of the trip to *not* answer it, which allowed Moxie to put her mind on other things, like what she was going to do with Billy J once she got him back to Santa Sofia.

"Where are Dodie and Kate?" Billy J asked when Moxie slipped into his room alone, let the door fall shut, leaned back against it and eased out a sigh of relief.

"I sent them to the cafeteria to get coffee so you and I could be alone."

"I've been alone plenty this past week." He grabbed at the railing on his bed to help him sit up, then he arranged the sheets nice and smooth over his noticeably smaller belly.

He still had on his hospital gown and the little plastic band around his wrist with all his vital information on it, but today for the first time since he'd been here, he had on his captain's hat with the parrot feather in it. Plus, the old twinkle had returned to his eyes.

Still, he had to pause for a few abrupt coughs as he announced, "I'm ready for a little lively company."

"Okay, I sent them to the cafeteria because *I* needed some space." She came in and plunked down on the empty bed beside his. "And by the way, if you said that to make me feel guilty, it won't work. I visited you every day you were in here."

"I know that, honey." He waved off her bad mood with one meaty hand then laughed. "So did Dodie."

"She did?"

"Didn't she tell you?"

"We, uh, I haven't seen her all week."

"All week? How much more space do you need than that?"

Moxie squirmed. "I just . . . It's this whole instant family thing. It's just overwhelming. I'm used to my independence. I'm used to having to rely only on myself."

"That's my doing."

"I didn't mean it as an accusation."

"I know, sweetheart, but still . . ."

"And you weren't the only parent involved in making me who I am, in case you hadn't noticed."

"Oh, I noticed." He reached out to her.

She got up and came to him.

When she laid her hand in his, he engulfed it in both of his. "All through that first year after Linda left, you probably felt like I didn't notice anything but my own anger and humiliation and grief. I tried my best to hide it from you but now I realize that probably only made things worse."

He had thought he'd done her a favor by doing that. Sparing her having to see and perhaps share in his emotional turmoil after his marriage fell apart. For the first time in years she saw her father in a different light. A more human light: More vulnerable.

"It was a tough time for both of us," she said softly. "But that actually wasn't what I meant when I said I learned to rely on myself alone."

"What do you mean then?"

"I meant that I was right here all the time." She found herself putting the pieces together as she talked it through. "You came and went. The Cromwells came and went, even though we didn't know who they were. Linda just went. And I stayed here. I was always *right here*. In Santa Sofia."

"Where anyone could have found you." Her father's mouth puckered into a pensive frown.

"If they had only looked," Moxie whispered.

If they had only looked! It was the first time Moxie had ever said, out loud, anything even remotely akin to blaming the Cromwell family for their prolonged separation.

"*That's* what this is all about, isn't it?" Billy J tipped his hat to the back of his head and let his hand rest on his beet-red forehead. "You're not really all that overwhelmed by Dodie and the girls trying to get close to you *now*. This is about all the years up until now."

Moxie had reached the very same conclusion moments before her father gave it voice. For that she was glad, as she found, when she tried to speak again, her own voice had grown thin and quavering. "They were *close* to me all those years, Dad. All those years when I was so unhappy and our home life was so strained."

"I know, sweetie." He held his hand to her again.

"All those years when I needed a mom and would have loved having sisters. They were so close." She ignored his hand and went to the bed and crawled up beside him as though she were six years old and scared by lightning. "They didn't come for me then but now they want me to come running with open arms whenever they feel like acting like one big happy family."

"They tried, honey. They tried to find you. You've seen the garden."

Moxie thought of the odd garden behind the cottage on Dream Away Bay Court. Souvenirs from all over the country told the story of every place Dodie had tracked down stories of where her husband and kidnapped child might have gone. Not a single one of those artifacts reflected the obvious—not a one of them was from the local area.

She laid her head on his large, rounded shoulder and shut her eyes. "They didn't try hard enough."

"Oh, Molly Christina, my sweet little lost lamb, you think a day goes by that I don't tell myself that exact same thing?"

Moxie's eyes flew open and she bolted up. Her lips pressed together preparing, automatically, to call the stricken-faced woman standing in the doorway *Mom*. She caught herself before the word got out. "Dodie! I didn't mean for you to hear that."

"You don't have to say it out loud for me to get your message, Molly Chris—that is, Moxie, dear." The woman stood in the doorway with her hands folded in absolute stillness in front of her flouncy blue dress. Shadow disguised the expression on her face but she did nothing to hide the raw edge of her pain when she spoke. "You've made your feelings about me quite clear."

Moxie wanted to protest that she didn't even know what her feelings were, but she couldn't. Even though she had not analyzed and named her emotions, she had made quite clear, and quite often, the fact that she wasn't happy.

"I'm sorry. It's just . . ." She blinked and tears clung to her lashes. She tightened her jaw, willing them not to fall. "I just don't know how to act, how to react to all of this. You always knew what was missing in *your* life."

"I knew," Dodie said softly, placing her hand over her heart. "Heaven help me I never forgot it, not even for a day."

235

"But *I* didn't know. I had no idea I had any blood relatives." She turned to her father still looking pale and weak lying on the hospital bed. "Not that my foster family didn't give me—"

"A whale of a time?" Billy J joked, followed with a wheezing laugh.

"All the love in the world," she said. She laid the back of her hand over his flushed cheek. "Then that world fell apart."

Billy J's usually jovial face went somber.

"And I learned to cope with things on my own." She glanced at Dodie, wanting to assert her independence. She turned to her father, wanting to make sure she didn't come off haughty and ungrateful. "I never doubted how much you loved me, Daddy, but when the going got tough—"

"I went fishing."

Moxie could only nod at that.

"And I stayed out of your life far too long," he admitted, his eyes downcast.

"I managed. Thrived even." She touched the brim of his hat then gave the parrot feather a flick to lighten the mood and help illustrate her own resilience. "It wasn't an ideal situation but it made me who I am."

"Just like losing you made us who we are." Kate stepped into the doorway, putting her hand on Dodie's shoulder. "You aren't the only one questioning how to cope with these new relationships, Moxie."

"I know that. Don't you think I know that?" Moxie snapped at her sister's intrusion. "It's just harder for me because of my past."

Kate glared at Moxie.

Moxie glared right back.

"Mom always emphasized to Jo and me that sisterhood is not a competition. That we should be ourselves but never to forget to be sweet. I always thought she oversimplified things, but now I get it." Kate limped around her mother, her eyes never leaving Moxie's as she moved fully into the room. "Mom wanted us to always remember that no matter what we think we know about each other, underneath it all is a person who may be hurting to her very core. Who may feel lost, or scared, or so angry that it could affect the most significant choices she makes."

Some of the tension left Moxie's body as she considered that.

"She wanted us to love and cherish others because she understood better than anyone how quickly everything can change."

"I didn't have the benefit of that guidance, though, did I?" Moxie shifted her focus from Katie's defiant gaze to Dodie's tentative one. "I didn't have you."

"You have me now, baby." Her hand fluttered forward for only a second before she withdrew it again. "If you want me in your life, you have me now."

"And if I *don't* want you?"

"Moxie!" Billy J spoke with such force it set off a coughing fit.

Moxie went to him to pat his back. "Daddy, I'm not saying that to be cruel. I sincerely want to know. Not every situation like this comes with its own fairy-tale ending."

He shook his head, his gaze empathetic.

She turned to Dodie and Kate and asked the real question that had gnawed at her heart all this time. "What if I can't find a way to accept a new mom and sisters?"

Moxie did not know what she wanted Dodie to say, but she knew on a deeper level that it could well set the tone for everything that happened between them from now on.

"I can only speak for myself." Dodie stepped forward. She did not let her gaze waver from her youngest daughter, even when her footsteps faltered slightly and her voice trembled with emotion. "If you can't find room in your heart to accept me as your mom then . . ."

Then I'll leave.

Moxie braced herself. Everyone's always left. Her birth father, her foster mother. She lived in a town based on people coming into your life for a very short time then leaving again. When she had finally found a man who she thought she could fall in love with, he did not plan to stay.

"Go on," she urged. "Say it."

238

"Then I will respect your feelings."

She knew it! Moxie exhaled and started for the door, needing to get some fresh air.

When she came shoulder to shoulder with Dodie, the older woman turned, only slightly, and with her eyes still fixed on Moxie said almost inaudibly, "But it won't change mine."

"What?" Moxie came to a halt beside Dodie.

"Molly Christina . . . Molly . . . my sweet, sweet baby girl. I could no sooner stop loving you than I could stop loving Kate or Jo. You are my child. You always have been and you always will be."

Moxie was moved but it had only hinted at the answer she knew was coming. "I'm not a child. What if I can't deal with all this as an adult?"

She was pushing. She knew it but she couldn't stop herself. She had to push. She had to know if Dodie would do what her birth father and foster mom had done—leave.

"If you'd come back when I was a kid, maybe I could have made the adjustment more easily but you didn't. And I don't know if I can. If only . . ."

"That's enough of that." Dodie held her hand up to cut Moxie off. "I love you too much to stand here and let you drag yourself down with that kind of talk."

"I just said . . ."

Kate held up a finger and warned, with quiet compassion, "For once maybe you should listen instead of shooting off your mouth about what

239

you want or what you think. This is one thing Mom knows a little something about."

Moxie pressed her lips together and glowered at Kate.

"You may not have grown up with me advising you about sisterhood or understanding anyone you meet might harbor a hurting heart, but I can share this with you now. 'If only' isn't going to help you, make you a better person or change a thing about the past." Dodie took Moxie's hand lightly. "I learned not long after you were taken that those are some of the heaviest words in the English language. Some people use them like an anchor to keep their lives always in the past."

If only my birth family had found me sooner. If only my foster mother had cared more about her family than herself. If only . . .

Moxie felt the pull of the words instantly, weighing her down, triggering unproductive emotions as she thought of her own list of grievances.

"I could not afford to do that," Dodie went on. "I could not move forward and do what I had to do—be a mother to Jo and Kate and never stop searching for you—I couldn't do any of that dragging 'if only' along with me."

Just as, moments earlier, she had seen her father—her daddy, her hero—not in those terms but in all his humanity, she now saw Dodie. Not as just another vulnerable, sometimes daffy older woman trying to push her own needs onto her newly found daughter, but as a single mom who put her own pain aside in order to do what had to be done. Not larger than life but bigger than the heartache life had dealt her.

"What does that mean? I'm not sure how to—"

"It means I only know how to live in the now." Dodie gripped Moxie's hand more tightly now. "If you tell me that you can't accept me as your mother then I will deal with that."

"And leave?" If Dodie wasn't going to say it, Moxie would.

"Leave?" Dodie scoffed. "Oh, no, sweetheart, I would never leave."

"Even if I didn't want to be a daughter to you?"

"Even if you didn't want to speak to me. Or see me. Even if you told everyone in town to shun me. I would stay right here."

"Stay?" Moxie didn't know how to react to that. "And do what?"

"I wouldn't try to force you to change your mind, if that's what you're asking." The older woman's eyes were damp. "I guess I would just wait and hope and pray that time and love would change your heart."

"You'd . . . stay?" Moxie couldn't get over it. Nobody stayed. Nobody just waited and prayed for her. They ran off. They went fishing. They did not . . . "Stay. But why?"

"I lost you once." Dodie raised her free hand to caress Moxie's cheek. "I will *never* lose you again."

Moxie tried not to break out crying like a baby, tried to play it cool. But the second her lower lip quivered and Dodie brushed a tear off her cheek, she fell into her mother's arms at long last and lost herself in a deep hug. "Oh, Mom!"

"Molly Chris—"

"No, that's okay. I kind of like it when you call me that."

"Molly." Tears flooded Dodie's eyes. "My Molly Christina. After all these years, you are finally really a part of our family again at last."

When Moxie pulled away she had one more question she had to ask. "Why? Why if I didn't want anything to do with you, would you have stayed?"

"Because that's what families do," Kate whispered as she joined her mother and sister in their hug.

Moxie shook her head. "So families go *and* families stay?"

"Families do what needs to be done," Dodie said.

"I think I'm going to like being a part of the family." Moxie sniffled. "Now we just have one more issue to resolve."

"What's that?" Kate wanted to know.

"Now that we've worked out what being in this family means, how do we keep this family together? Mom, how will we stay close to Jo and Kate if they leave Santa Sofia?"

"I'm not going anywhere." Kate raised her hand as if giving her pledge.

Dodie reached for her older daughter to hug her, too. "Oh, Katie, you don't have to do that, not when you finally—"

She shook her head. "No more Scat-Kat Katie."

"But Vince?" Moxie asked.

"If Vince chases after Gentry then that's where his heart is, that's who his family is, and it won't include me. I understand that. As long as he puts his grown child ahead of his own future and moving on, there won't be any room for me."

Moxie reached out and put her arm around Kate. "I've known Vince a long time. Don't give up on him too soon."

"I won't. Not this time. But I won't run away again—I have obligations to Mom and you and Lionel and my work and myself. I plan to stay here."

"So Mom is staying. You are staying. I am . . ." What if Hunt asked her to go away with him when he leaves? Moxie shook her head. Getting a little ahead of herself, wasn't she? "I am staying."

"If only Jo . . ." Kate murmured.

"Uh-uh," Dodie warned.

243

Moxie laughed. "I wouldn't worry too much about Jo."

"But she seems to have fallen so easily back into her old life in Atlanta. Why would she come back to Santa Sofia?"

"Because Santa Sofia has one thing Atlanta never will."

"Us?" Dodie asked.

"The Bait Shack!" Billy J proclaimed.

Kate folded her arms. "Are you thinking—"

"The one thing Santa Sofia has that Atlanta never will is Travis Brandt," Moxie concluded. "And I think it's about time Travis did a little outreach for the chapel, don't y'all?"

Chapter Twenty-One

"I've been thinking a lot about what we talked about Friday night." Vince found Kate in what had become their usual Sunday-morning pew in the Traveler's Wayside Chapel.

"And?" She tipped her head back, her pulse picking up in anticipation that he would say he'd hashed out his issues and wanted to stay in Santa Sofia. Preferably with her as his wife.

He paused, looked around the chapel, which had just opened its doors and wouldn't start services for almost twenty minutes, then gave a half-hearted shrug. "I don't know what to say."

"And yet your lips are moving." She rolled her eyes, finding it hard to believe he had stopped to speak to her just to say nothing.

She flounced her full cotton skirt in an attempt to get it to lift perfectly over her cast and to let him know her interest in his uncertainty had waned.

"I just . . . Can I sit?" He edged forward.

She gave him a look but what could she do? They were in church after all. She tucked her injured foot out of the way as best she could and wedged herself into the corner created by the end of the pew to allow Vince to get by her.

"I'm glad you're here early," he told her. "I was afraid by the time I got Fabbie settled in the nursery I'd have to take a seat in the back by myself."

He dropped down so close and so hard that the lace trim on the hem of her white, frilly skirt flipped up. She smoothed it down not because it had revealed even an inch of leg but because . . . because she *wanted* to. It sent a message. She wasn't sure what message and she had no illusion that Vince picked up on it anyway, so it wasn't really a clear or effective message. But then that seemed to be exactly the kind of message best suited for their relationship.

Pseudo relationship? Nonpermanent, nonrelationship? She didn't even know how to think of them anymore. All she knew was that after she had left his home Friday night he had stayed on her mind and their situation weighed on her heart every minute.

He hadn't even called.

"Sorry," he said as he fiddled with his bulletin, adjusted his tie then took a quick look around them. Even though nobody seemed to be looking at them and not even the musical prelude had begun to tell the congregation to quiet down, he employed the classic shoulder to shoulder, whispering out of the side of his mouth as he spoke to her. "I missed you yesterday. Thought you'd come by after helping out with Billy J."

"I guess that took longer than I anticipated." All too true.

She had opted to go to help get Billy J at the hospital instead of pitching in with Fabbie on Saturday to give herself some time and perspective. Of course, the way that turned out, she was glad she went along, but even so, she had not counted on the simple errand being an all-day task.

Waiting for the doctor to show up to sign the order took until early afternoon. The prolonged and often comedic effort to get all the flowers and plants, sent by Santa Sofians and regulars from the Bait Shack, into Dodie's car so that they and the human cargo could all survive the trip home without coming uprooted ate up another hour. Getting Billy J situated and comfy at Moxie's place was no small accomplishment, either.

"If you'd have called and asked me, I'd have come over after we got him home. Though, it took all three of us to keep the old boy from throwing on a Hawaiian shirt, some khaki shorts and tennis shoes and heading down to the Bait Shack to make sure everything was all right."

Vince laughed. "You should have called for backup."

She gave him a sidelong glance, realizing he

had a good point. She'd been so fixated on him not calling her that she hadn't even considered calling him, even when they all could have benefited from it. He'd have done a much better job at keeping the boisterous old boy in line than three doting ladies who waffled between scolding and babying him. "I didn't think of that."

"And after that big speech we all gave Moxie at the clinic about dropping everything to come help when it's needed?"

About *family* dropping everything and coming. She tried not to read more into his leaving that out. "You had your own hands full with Fabbie. We certainly wouldn't want you to have dropped her."

"Especially just for such a losing proposition as talking sense into Billy J Weatherby." Moxie turned around from the pew in front of them.

"It's not polite to eavesdrop," Kate reminded her.

"Who's eavesdropping? I'm family, remember? I'm just including myself in the conversation." She smiled broadly.

"It's not so much a conversation as an explanation," Vince volunteered. "Kate was just letting me know why she left me high and dry taking care of Fabbie yesterday after she promised to—"

"Oh, no." Kate twisted in the pew to face him. "You are not laying that at my doorstep."

"Huh?" Moxie crooked her arm over the back to the pew so she could not only join the conversation but actually insinuate herself into it physically.

"What are you trying to say, Kate?" Vince asked quietly.

"I'm saying that I've said goodbye to Scat-Kat Katie. Goodbye to the girl who runs at the first hint of genuine commitment. That's not me anymore. I thought I made that clear when I left Friday, Vince. I said I would come by to honor my promise to take care of Fabbie, *if* you needed me to. You didn't call. I got the message. *You don't need me.*"

"Kate, I never said—"

"Just don't try to make my not helping you out yesterday about me. It was you, Vince. From this point forward whatever happens to our relationship is your call." Kate pushed up from her seat and used a combination of lunging and lurching to get herself into the pew next to Moxie.

"It's not me, Kate. If only it were just me and you, I'd be on one knee right now."

Kate thought that should have excited, or at least comforted, her more. *If only . . .*

She jerked her shoulders taut. "This is neither the time nor the place for this, Vince."

"Are you kidding? This is Wayside Chapel, Kate, not some fancy 'everybody hush up and sit still' kind of church," Moxie whispered. "This is the kind of place where people come to be fed spiritually and physically. If you can't speak honestly and openly here, then you two don't stand a chance of ever working this out."

Kate looked up at the large driftwood cross hanging above the simple candlelit altar. "Who says we stand a chance of working this out?"

"The man just said he would get down on his knee for you." Moxie punched Kate lightly in the arm then jerked her head toward Vince.

He had, hadn't he? The full impact of that hit her at last. Kate whipped her own head around to look directly at him.

"But it's not just you and me, Kate. I can't make any kind of plans much less proposals until Gentry makes up his mind whether to take that job in Miami or not."

"See?" Kate glared at Moxie, too humiliated to even look in Vince's direction. "You should stay out of other people's business."

"Sounds like Moxie isn't the only one who feels cramped by having your family always so close at hand," Vince mumbled.

"No kidding. Apparently Gentry does, too," Moxie snapped.

Kate raised her hand to quiet her sister but Vince scooted to the edge of his pew and demanded, "What do you mean by that?"

"Well, let's see. Gentry has only just begun managing his life without your intervention, financially or otherwise, for a couple of months now, right?"

Vince kept his lips pressed tightly together and gave a curt nod.

"And already he's job hunting in another city?" Moxie made a motion with her hand which indicated he should draw his own conclusion from that.

"You think he's doing that to run away from me?"

"No, sweetie." Kate touched his arm. "He's not running. Take it from an expert on that subject. He's just . . . He's trying . . . He needs . . ."

"He needs to create a little space to build a life for himself. You're suffocating him and that messes with his relationship with Pera and Fabbie. He'd never want to hurt you, but he has to put his wife and child first."

"I was getting to that part," Kate told her sister. "I just wanted to word it a bit more diplomatically."

"You can thank me for my bluntness later." Moxie crinkled her nose.

"Is this true?" Vince asked.

"Yes, she's quite blunt." Kate gave Moxie a one-eyed squint.

"About Gentry," Vince said softly.

"Vince." She slid her hand down his arm and gripped his hand in hers. "You know the answer to that."

He had to know it. If he didn't know it, if he didn't have just a deep-down inkling about it, then no one could ever convince him of it. "If you don't already have the answer to that question then you can't change. Even if you try to change, you'd always have that niggling feeling that you had been forced into a hasty decision."

He lifted his head at that. "Is that how you felt?"

"I don't—"

"When you took off and broke our engagement? Did you feel that I had pressured you based on my assumptions about what was best for us rather than letting you find your answers?"

"I suppose it was."

"You were pretty wise for a kid just out of college, Kate."

"Just out of college, yes, but a kid? I was never a kid, Vince. Not since the night . . ." Her gaze shifted to Moxie.

The younger sister put her hand on the older one's. "I'm just now understanding that living with what our birth father did closed in around you and Jo and Dodie far more than finding an instant family is cramping my lifestyle."

"Thank you for that," Kate said softly.

"Like I said, thank me later." Moxie scooted over to nudge Kate over. "Right now, you have work to do."

"Work?"

Moxie moved closer still.

Kate thought of pushing back against the younger sister. Or at least planting her cane solidly to hold her ground. But just then the music that told everyone to find a place and prepare themselves to worship the Lord started up. Kate put out her hand to protect her personal space as best she could. "Hey, get back over where you belong. You're crowding me here."

Kate gripped her cane and glowered at her younger sister.

"There is a man sitting one row back who said that if it were just you and him, he'd get down on one knee. And just about now he's probably realizing it is just you and him, because his son is a grown man with a wife and child, who doesn't need him tagging along when he goes out to make his way in life." Moxie gestured toward Vince. "So why don't you get back there where it will be just you and him?"

"Because he . . . I . . ." Kate glanced over her shoulder.

Vince tipped his head to encourage her to join him.

"I'll move," Kate said to Moxie then added to Vince, "But it's not because I can't commit."

"That's too bad because I was thinking about how much I'd like you to do just that."

"Move?"

He smiled, stood to help her work her way around to sit beside him, leaned in and whispered, "Commit."

Her knees almost buckled.

He held her up then helped her sit.

"Vince, are you . . . ?"

He sat beside her. "This is the place where people speak the truth and work through their issues, Kate. I may not have all our issues worked out—"

"Yet."

"Yet," he concurred. "But the truth is that I love you. I don't think I ever stopped loving you."

"I feel the same way. I love you, Vince."

The music came to an end and everyone stood. Vince got up from the pew first, then turned and held out his hand.

Kate put her fingers in his and reached for her cane, but before she could get it, Vince moved it aside.

"I need—"

Vince dropped to one knee in front of her.

She held her breath.

The music swelled but when the time came for everyone to begin singing not a single voice rose in song.

"Kate Cromwell . . ." Vince took her hand, not seeming to care that everyone in the place started gaping at them.

The music stopped.

Travis, who had come out to stand by the

informal altar, held his hands up to tell everyone to stay as they were, in essence giving them license to gape and ogle all they wanted.

Vince gave a nod to Travis then to the congregation before turning back to Kate. He looked up at her, his eyes hopeful and a huge smile on his face. "Kate Cromwell . . ."

"You said that part already," someone called from the group.

"Thanks." He gave them a wave then fixed his eyes on her again. "Will you marry me?"

Suddenly Kate didn't care about the stares, either.

"Oh, Vince!" She threw her arms around him.

"Is that a yes?" the same person wanted to know.

"Yes," she murmured into his ear for him alone before she pulled away from him and shouted for all to hear, "Yes!"

A cheer went up.

The pianist played the opening chords of "The Wedding March."

Travis held his hands up to get everyone's attention. "Before we sing our opening hymn, let's all join in a moment of prayer for the happy couple."

The happy couple. At last.

They prayed together and when they raised their voices to sing, Kate looked up at Vince.

He slipped his arm around her waist and smiled at her.

She stole a peek at Moxie and mouthed a thank-you.

Moxie touched two fingers to her lips and blew her a kiss just the way an adoring kid sister would to her big sister.

Kate grinned and when her gaze fell on Travis she thought of Jo. Then she thought of Moxie and their mom wanting to find a way to reach out to the middle Cromwell sister and hopefully bring her home. Suddenly Kate wanted that, too, more than anything.

And she had an idea how to nudge that along.

Chapter Twenty-Two

The open house started in less than an hour.

Jo had planned to arrive much earlier but when she got up this morning she'd felt the tug to go to church. Her intellect kept nagging: too much to do, too little time. But her heart listened to another voice. That voice convinced her with the reminder that she could never hope to make a fresh start if she fell back into serving her old priorities.

So she made time to attend her former church and trusted the rest of her dealings, with debt, Mike Powers and the house, would wait.

After that, she had made a quick stop at a grocery store to pick up a tube of cookie dough. It was an old Realtor trick and one she normally didn't employ, but with the house devoid of anything but the basic furnishings that she could beg or borrow on short notice, she really needed something to give the place a homey touch.

Of course in doing all this she had forgotten about Atlanta traffic, which wasn't too awfully bad on a Sunday, and hadn't accounted for the distance. She'd spent the past two months living in a small town that only took a matter of minutes to move through and had lost her edge for driving in a real city.

Jo pulled to a stop by the large sign at the entrance to the subdivision. She'd just get the signage up to advertise the open house then get down to the property to bake the cookies and see to any last-minute . . .

"Balloons?" Jo pulled up short just inches shy of tripping over the familiar Mike Powers Realty open house sign. The sign that had not been there when she finally dragged herself away from working on the house at 2:00 a.m. this morning. She had neither placed it there nor authorized anyone else to put it in the common area to lead people to the house she so needed to sell.

"This can't be right." She stood back to check the street address again. It was her house all right. "What's going on here?"

She didn't know, but the suspicions it aroused in her made her stomach hurt.

She hurried back to her car and wound her way back through the upscale new subdivision to the house where she had spent almost every waking hour since returning to Atlanta. She parked in front and took a cautious look around before getting out from behind the wheel.

No cars in the drive. No sign of anyone on the premises. Nothing amiss at all, except . . .

Jo squinted at the door. She was sure she had locked up using the standard key box that Powers Realty kept on all its houses. Someone must have come by, posted the sign, gone in the house and left it unlocked.

"Not good." She took out her phone. Maybe Mike could clear things up. Though, if Mike knew anything, surely he'd have let her know. "Not good at all."

She glanced at her phone and hoped she'd find an explanation waiting for her in her messages.

She pushed the button and all thoughts of explanations fell away.

"Travis," she whispered. One. Two. Three. Four. Five missed calls but only one voice mail.

"Hey, Jo. Just wanted to call and tell you . . . I miss you. I mean, I . . . I really miss you."

She bit her lower lip but she could not rein in a broad, spontaneous smile.

"Anyway, there's more than just that but it's not 'leave a message and get back to me' kind of stuff. I'll try to call again. I can't wait to talk to you."

She brushed her fingertip down the face of her phone. "I can't wait to talk to you, either."

Which made it all the more imperative that she get this house sold and get back to her real life. She put her hand on the driver's-side door handle and paused long enough to check her phone for any other messages. Not a one.

She got out of the car, fished her supplies out of the backseat and marched up to the door. She had a spare key but for her own satisfaction she had to try to turn the handle. It would be locked. She knew it.

The handle turned without a hint of resistance. Jo gasped.

The heavy door swung open.

She held her phone up, trying to think who to call for help, or *if* she should call for help.

A shaft of sunlight hit the gleaming tile floor and created an almost-blinding glare into which stepped . . .

"Oh!"

"What are you doing opening the door at my open house?"

"I thought you were Brittney," the young girl explained.

"I thought *you* were Brittney." Jo didn't know *which* Brittney but she felt certain it was one of Mike's eager young protégés.

"I *am*," the girl explained. "I thought you were the other Brittney."

"Why in the world would you think that?" Jo asked.

"Because *I'm* here." *Duh.* She didn't say that, or whatever young women her age said now to make it clear they are less than impressed with someone, but her expression got the point across.

260

Jo folded her arms. She'd gone through too much, paid far too many dues in this business to find herself cowed by a younger, less polite version of herself circa ten years ago. She stepped over the threshold. "Just tell me why you're here."

"Mike set it up for us. He said we could use the practice." Brittney gave the door a push and it closed with a bang. "We've done all the prep work and Brittney will be here any minute with our handouts on this place."

"First, you did not do all the prep work on this house. I have been here nonstop since I got here." Jo winced. Even Brittney had to know what she'd meant by that.

"Oh, yeah? Well . . ." Jo imagined hearing the little marble that rolled along the tracks of the kid's train of thought sliding from one side of her brain to the other. "Yeah, well, so have I," Brittney insisted.

If Jo had had a free hand she'd have rubbed her forehead. Not that the action would ease the slow throbbing beginning to build behind her eyes but it might send a signal to the girl that she had reached the end of her patience. The stress of all this had definitely begun to get to her.

"Only I got here first." Yes, it came out sounding childish, but Jo didn't care. She did not miss a step, just swept onward clutching her grocery bag and satchel in one hand and her keys and phone in the other. She still had so much left to do before people started showing up. *If* people started showing up.

She had worked so hard, spending money she didn't really have in order to get this place ready, but with no promise she would have any interest at all any time soon. Still, she had to try. She had to take care of things. She glanced down at the phone again then at Brittney, tagging along behind her. "Mike's arrangements for you to practice on this open house were made before I came back. Now—"

"No, they weren't."

Jo froze. "What do you mean?"

"Brittney and I talked to him this morning and Mike said we should come ahead and do the open house. He mentioned you were all religious and wouldn't work on a Sunday so it wouldn't step on your toes."

"Step on my toes?"

"Yeah, I thought that was a weird thing to say, too. I mean, if you aren't even here, how could we step on your . . . Hey, great shoes!"

Jo glanced down at the peep-toe black with white trim Italian leather pumps she had slipped on just to give her a confidence boost for this open house. She'd found them among her things in the storage unit she and Kate and their mom had rented for things they hadn't been able to get to Santa Sofia yet. She hadn't gone there looking for shoes or for remnants of her life in Atlanta.

She'd gone to see what she could make use of to decorate the house, but when she'd seen the neat little stacks of boxes, all sporting the labels of really expensive shoes, she'd given into temptation and donned a pair.

"Thank you," she murmured, not above pointing her toe and rolling her ankle to one side to show every angle of her prized footwear.

"You must have made a ton of money doing this." Brittney's eyes glittered with newfound respect.

"Uh-huh." She let out a nervous but pleased-with-herself laugh. No harm in taking credit for years of hard work, she thought.

"Then why'd you leave?"

Jo pulled her foot in, took a breath and reached for her satchel. "Because while I may have made a ton of money, I lost a whole lot more than that."

"Yeah, the stories about *this* money pit are, like, legendary." The girl retreated to clear the way for Jo to walk past.

Jo stopped and met this Brittney eye to eye. "When I said I lost more I didn't mean money. Oh, not that I didn't lose a lot of that. Technically, because I'm in debt, I'm still losing money on this property."

"That's lousy luck."

"I don't believe in luck, Brittney. Everyone thinks I was blindsided by the foundering housing market, but I got in this mess all by myself."

"Talk around the office is there are others you could blame."

"No." Jo shook her head. "I have to take responsibility. I got greedy, and not for money. I got greedy to *be* somebody."

"You?" She looked completely baffled by the revelation. "You are somebody. You were, like, in magazines and on billboards."

"That wasn't me, Brittney."

"It wasn't?"

"Not the real me." Jo put her hand to her chest. "The real me is a geeky, lonely kid who just wanted people to like her. If not like her then at least *notice* her." She put her hand on the shoulder of the pretty young woman. "Not that I think you'll understand that."

The girl's whole demeanor softened toward Jo. Her gaze dropped for a second, she fiddled with her hair before looking Jo in the eyes and saying, "Oh, I understand."

"You do?"

"I worked as a receptionist for a competing Realty company ever since I got out of high school. When you're a receptionist you kind of become invisible to people, especially successful people and stressed-out people. You probably don't know how *that* feels."

Jo couldn't recall ever feeling any other way. Oh, wait, yes, she could.

When Travis looked at her.

"You'd be surprised what I know, Brittney." She gave the girl's shoulder a squeeze then dropped her hand.

She smiled a bit shyly then raised one shoulder in a halfhearted shrug. "Anyway, when you're invisible like that, people say things in front of you like you weren't even there."

Jo nodded.

"You see their mail. You know who calls them and how often." She licked her lips and glanced out the still-open front door nervously. "You figure out things."

"Ah." She was trying to tell Jo something. She suddenly felt bad about her private joke about that lone marble. "What have you figured out, Brittney?"

"That you'd better watch out for Mr. Powers."

That sent a chill through Jo from her scalp to her peep-toed toes. "What do you—"

"Hey, what's going on?" The other Brittney came in with her own grocery bag dangling from her arm.

"Turn around," the Brittney in front of Jo told the Brittney behind her. "We're not staying."

"We're not? Why not?" The other one wanted to know.

"Because it's not our house to show." Brittney pointed firmly toward the door.

"But this was going to be our lucky break." The protest came back over the sound of a plastic grocery sack crinkling.

"I don't believe in luck." Brittney looked directly at Jo. "We were sent out here for some reason that had nothing to do with getting a break. In fact, I think we've been used, Britt."

"So? That's part of the game, right?"

"If we want to get into real estate, we should take responsibility for ourselves and do this right."

"We did it right." The protest took on a whiny tone.

"Oh, come on!" Brittney put her hands on her slender hips. "I worked six weeks as a receptionist for Powers Realty then the big boss says he thinks I can do more, he hires you and two weeks later with only a few hours of training we're showing the business's biggest problem property?"

The other girl's eyes narrowed. She tipped her heart-shaped chin up. "He said we could be somebody."

Jo looked at the girl in front of her and smiled. "Does he have that printed on his business cards?"

Brittney giggled.

"Thanks, kiddo." Jo set her things on the floor, stepped forward and gave the young woman a quick hug. "I won't ask you to tell me more. You still need a job in the morning."

"I will. But that doesn't mean I won't start looking for another one as soon as I can." Brittney hugged her back.

"If you need shoes to give you confidence for the job hunt, give me a call."

Brittney pulled back and shook her head. "Those are cool but I think they come at too high a price."

"Smart girl," Jo whispered. She stepped back and watched the young woman go by. When the pair of them reached the door, she called out. "If it wouldn't jeopardize your job to tell me—nobody is going to show up for this open house, are they?"

She paused and looked at her friend. She gnawed her lower lip for a moment then squared her shoulders and said, "People could show up. Mike had us put signs up all over today."

"All over but he didn't run print ads or get it in the paper. Weird, huh?" the other girl offered.

Mysterious phone calls taken outside the office. Receptionists promoted to Realtors-in-training for one poorly executed open house, *hers*.

When she arrived and messed up his plan, Mike suddenly came up with some money to firm up his claim of partnership on the deal. Not to mention that whole cake nonsense. Jo looked around. "I don't suppose either of you brought that cake here that he had you go get Friday?"

"That's another weird thing," the newer girl volunteered. "He had us put it in the break room and when it got down to just a couple pieces and globs of leftover icing, he took it away."

Jo nodded. "The pieces are coming together now."

"The pieces of the cake are coming together?" Britt asked Brittney. "I don't get it."

"You're better off not getting it for now," Brittney assured her. "We have to go."

"You girls go on. I'll man the open house." Jo kicked off her shoes.

Brittney gave her a look of surprise at that.

"I have a lot of questions. I plan to stay here until I get my answers." Jo smiled and shrugged. "I might as well be comfortable. Those shoes just don't fit me anymore."

Chapter Twenty-Three

One hour into the two-hour open house and not a single house hunter. Not even the usual neighbors dropping in to snoop around out of boredom or curiosity. Jo had expected as much.

Mike did, too. In fact, he had planned for it.

It had only taken her a few minutes to put the pieces of his latest scheme together.

Jo walked through the empty shell of a house. They'd bought it for way less than cost when the home owner had declared bankruptcy after living in it less than a year.

"What a steal," Mike had said. "It needs work but has good bones. Just a few tricks and tweaks and we rake in a big, easy profit."

"A steal," Jo murmured. She ran her hand along the door that led from the kitchen to the basement steps. For the first time since she'd made the deal last spring, she noticed the faint pencil marks on the door frame.

Daddy. The slash a few inches higher than Jo's head.

Mommy. About Jo's eye level.

Zoey. Not quite to Jo's waist.

Jakers. Eight inches? She didn't know if Jakers was a baby or the family pet.

It didn't matter, really. The key word in the whole equation was *family*.

"A steal," she murmured again. They hadn't made a steal of a deal, they had stolen a home. A home from Daddy, Mommy, Zoey and even Jakers. Forget the good bones of the house; like financial vultures they had picked clean the bones of a family. For no other reason than their shot at raking in a big profit using tricks and tweaks.

Sure, the family had to bear the responsibility of whatever choices or actions led to the point of such loss, but Jo could not excuse her part.

She thought of Moxie for a moment. Basically they did the same kind of work. Only Moxie helped families find homes, helped her beloved hometown keep the families it needed to stay viable. Moxie bought and sold and rented property that she looked after herself because she cared about the people and the places.

Jo could have done the same. Or something close to it. Plenty of Realtors stayed out of the house-flipping business. Why didn't she?

Why are you doing what you are doing? Who are you trying to serve?

The essence of Travis's questions to her. He said she must answer those things before she could start a ministry at the chapel or before they could begin their life together.

Why had she done what she did, pursued the fast buck, often at someone else's expense and sometimes with less than the best intentions regarding a fast resale?

Jo was good at her work. She was a good Realtor. But house flipping? She had never done anything illegal. Or even unethical, really. But she should have held herself to a higher standard, to be a good Christian. Except, back then, she hadn't really understood what that entailed.

She had just wanted to impress Mike, to be somebody in his eyes. In *anyone's* eyes.

How could she have let her own insecurities lead her so far away from the truth she had always claimed to know? How could she have forgotten?

She was always someone in God's eyes.

No matter what shoes she wore. How much money she made. Who loved her, or noticed her or even ignored her. She was always someone in God's eyes.

Which led her to the next question.

Who are you trying to serve?

Jo closed her eyes. Up until probably these past few days she had still been trying to serve her own needs, enslaved to her own fears. But once she had gotten here, once she had thrown herself into the work in this house, once she had looked at Brittney this morning and understood that everybody feels invisible and unloved at one time or another, it all changed.

She let her fingertips linger on the slash marks a moment longer. "Wherever they are, Father, be with this family and bless them."

She opened her eyes and blinked away the tears pooling above her lashes. She sniffled and went into the living room to find her shoes where she had left them.

That day on the beach she had fretted about not leaving footprints, not mattering. Now it all seemed so clear. Once she accepted how much she mattered to God she stopped worrying about leaving her mark. Once she placed her trust fully in the One who made the sand and the tide she'd no longer try to make people see her and start living in a way so that people saw God in her.

Yes. That was her answer. Her unfinished business wasn't this house, it was herself.

She reached for her phone and hit redial for the last caller. The call went straight to voice mail.

"Travis." She spoke softly but clearly in hopes that when he picked up, the message would come through in more than words. "Thank you," she whispered. "Thank you for getting me to come back to Atlanta and take a long, hard look at, well, everything. I think I have my answers now. For that alone, I'll always love you."

Love?

Jo startled at her own admission. She pulled the phone away from her ear, pressed the end call button and stared down at the dark screen. What had she done?

She knew she loved Travis, of course. Her mom knew, and Kate and Moxie. Actually, probably the whole town of Santa Sofia had reached that conclusion, perhaps even Travis himself. But she hadn't said it aloud to anyone yet.

She rubbed the pad of her thumb over the buttons. She could call back, claim the call had gotten cut off and give some kind of addendum or qualifier to her profession. *For that I'll always love your . . . super supportive, really great . . . method of . . . helping people to . . .*

"Fall totally, completely and undeniably in love with you." Jo spoke to the phone in her hand as though Travis himself were standing there. Or more aptly, as though he *weren't*. "Might as well face it, I said it. I meant it. If I called back I'd probably—"

"Say it again?"

Jo spun around to find Travis Brandt standing in the open doorway. Stunned, she could only murmur, "Make things worse."

"Uh-uh. Love doesn't make things worse, Jo. Not real love." He smiled.

Jo had missed that smile. It was the sun breaking over the beach after a starless, stormy night.

Say something, she told herself. Something wonderful and witty and poignant and perfect.

"Hi," she whispered.

"Hi, yourself." He looked around. "Can I come in?"

She swept her arm out the way she might invite a prospective buyer in. "It's an open house."

"Best kind," he said, coming toward her. "Don't you think?"

"Guess it depends on who walks through the door." She sank her teeth into her lower lip and watched as he approached her in his relaxed, confident way.

He came to her, reached out and stroked his fingers over her cheek, saying nothing.

Her lower lip slid from under her teeth. She tipped her head back. "It depends not just on who comes to your open house, but also why they came."

He lowered his head, his unwavering gaze searching her eyes.

Jo started to go up on her tiptoes to receive his kiss, then hesitated and put her hand on his chest. "Why *did* you come here?"

"I thought asking questions was my department." He leaned closer again.

Again she withdrew, just slightly. This time she turned her head so that his kiss fell on her temple. "Travis?"

274

He sighed and took a half step backward, his hands still on her arm and waist. "I told you. I missed you. I couldn't wait to see you."

She kept silent for a moment.

"Don't believe me?"

"Oh, I believe you all right. I just couldn't help thinking . . ."

"What?"

"That you've always seen me, Travis. From the first time we met you didn't just see a failed perfectionist with her hair all a mess and a freshly sprained ankle."

"Well, I could hardly miss that part."

"Yeah, but you also saw past it. That's why I thanked you in my voice mail. Why I thank God for bringing you into my life. You saw me not just as I was, but also as God wanted me to be. Because of that, I've actually started to become that person."

"It's not my handiwork, Jo."

She reached up and touched his face. "I have so much to tell you, Travis."

He turned his head and kissed her fingertips. "You've already told me the most important thing."

She gazed up at him earnestly. "That I've found my answers?"

"That you love me." He curled his fingers around her hand on his face, moved it away and leaned down. When his mouth was only inches away from hers he murmured, "I love you, too, Jo."

Heat flooded her cheeks. Her heart raced. "You do?"

He answered with a kiss.

"What are you doing in our house?" The strange man's booming voice startled them apart.

"*Your* house?" Travis looked from the man, woman and child standing in the doorway to Jo. "I thought this was *your* house."

"Are you the other buyer?" The woman clutched the child in her arms closer. Her head practically swiveled to look from Jo and Travis to the man standing next to her. When she spoke again her words came out in a panicked rush. "He said he had other buyers. I told you it wasn't a ploy. Nobody would be that awful, to know how much we want this house and make up another buyer just to drive the price up."

Jo's head swam. She felt sick to her stomach. "By he, you don't mean Mike Powers, do you?"

"Yeah." The man kept one hand on his wife's shoulder but his attention riveted on Jo. "Is that who you are working with, too? He pressed us to write a contract on the place last week, but we felt we had to pray about it. I guess you think that's kind of silly."

"Not at all." Jo glanced up at Travis. "In fact, I find it very touching and a little sad."

276

"Relying on prayer, sad?" the man asked, his hackles up.

"No, no!" Jo held her hands out to quell his uneasiness. "The way Mike has tried to manipulate you into making a decision on this house based on trickery and tweaks."

"Whatery and what?" Travis looked down at her.

"I'll explain it all later," she whispered to him, then turned to the couple, her hand extended. "I'm Jo Cromwell. I am the majority owner and agent of record on this property."

"You are very good at what you do," Travis said an hour later as he helped her go through the house, turning off lights and making notes of what furnishings they needed to collect and return before they headed back to Santa Sofia tomorrow.

"Thank you for excusing yourself while we dealt with the money issues, class act all the way." She handed him the box they would need to lock up when they finished up. "Even when the man realized you looked familiar and decided you must have gone to high school with his older brother!"

"Happens more often than you might think." He picked up her satchel in his free hand. "I've been out of the sportscasting public eye for long enough that people assume we have some kind of mundane personal connection when they can't quite place my face."

"I'd like you to place your face—" she went all coy and flirty as she gave her shoulders a waggle and tapped her index finger to her cheek "—right here."

"Actually, I was hoping for a less mundane kind of personal connection," he teased.

She turned to scold him and he leaned in and gave her a kiss on the lips. Nothing steamy enough to make him drop the lock or the satchel, but nice all the same.

"Thank you," she murmured.

"For a kiss? It was nothing. Feel free to ask me for one anytime." He grinned.

He had such a terrific grin. It complemented his sun-streaked hair and tanned face, giving him the hint of perpetual boyish charm, but in no way took away from the quiet strength of his masculine appeal.

"Not for the kiss, for the kick in the seat that got me back here."

"Kick in the seat? I think I'd have remembered if I'd done that."

"Speaking metaphorically." She laughed and took one look around. They had agreed to wait until Mike showed up with the last bits of the cake—planned to make the interested buyers think the open house had been well attended—but now, she thought maybe it would be better if they just let it go. "You gave me the motivation I needed to come back here and deal with all this. I guess that's just part of what you do as a man of the cloth?"

"It can be. Only I didn't do it as a man of the cloth."

"No?"

"I did it as a man." He set the satchel down and the lock on top of it, then stood up straight, his gaze on her face the whole time. "A man who very much wanted the woman he loved to be happy."

"I am hap— Did you say the woman he loved?"

He smiled.

She went to him. If she had put her shoes back on instead of leaving them lying in the middle of the front room, she'd have been tall enough to place her hands on his shoulders and look into his eyes. Instead, she flattened her palms on his chest and looked up at him. "Say it again."

"I love you, Jo."

Her heart thudded in her ears. She could barely breathe. "You do?"

"That's why I came here."

"It is?"

"Your mom and sisters may tell you at some point that it was because they put the idea in my head or that I came to tell you some good news that they obviously could have given you over the phone."

"Mom? What?" She tried to make sense of that last bit.

"Never mind. I'll tell you about that over dinner. It can wait, but this can't." He dropped to one knee before her.

Suddenly she was very glad to have discarded her shoes. If she had had them on, she'd have surely fallen off them right then and probably sprained both her ankles in the process.

"Travis! You don't mean . . . I thought you'd want some kind of proof that I had dealt with all my issues and—"

He put his finger to her lips. "The fact that you came here. The fact that you confronted your past, that you did it even though I knew you didn't want to, told me everything I needed to know. You say I always saw you, Jo. The truth is you always showed me who you were, from the first day we met when you greeted me with humor despite the pain of your sprained ankle. When your heart went out to the people who came in and out of the Wayside Chapel." He smiled up at her. "When you took charge of that deal just now and didn't care about hanging around to rub Mike Powers's nose in having caught him trying to skim whatever extra money he could off the sale of this place."

"Oh, Travis." She ran her fingers along his collar.

He reached into his pocket and produced a

280

simple but elegant diamond ring. "Jo, will you be my wife?"

Tears flooded her eyes. "Really?"

He laughed. "Yes, really."

"Then . . . yes. Really." She threw her arms around his neck. "I'll be your wife, Travis. And your helpmate and—"

He kissed her before she went down the whole list and when he looked into her eyes again, he slid the ring on her finger.

She took a second to admire it. "It's perfect."

"You're perfect," he murmured into her hair.

"Far from it, and don't you forget it," she warned.

He laughed and opened his mouth to say something but another man's voice intruded.

"What's going on here? Jo? Who is this? Where are—"

"The buyers have already gone, Mike." Jo stepped away from Travis, bent at the knees and took up her satchel and lock. "You'll have the contract for the house on your desk in the morning."

"Contract? Buyers? I don't . . ."

Jo could have launched into a long tirade telling the man just what she thought of him and his sneaky tactics. But she had just gotten engaged to the most wonderful man she knew and she didn't want to waste another fraction of her energy on Mike Powers ever again.

She headed for the door and when she got to it, and Mike, standing there with his partially eaten cake in hand, she paused. For a split second she thought about pushing the mess of icing and crumbs into his expensive blue suit but she couldn't do it.

"Here's the lock. Please make sure it's on the door when you leave. Remember if anything is missing or damaged Powers Realty will still be responsible." She pressed the black box into his hand and walked past.

"Nice to meet you." Travis walked out of the door behind her.

It wasn't until her bare feet hit the concrete that she remembered her shoes and she turned to rush back to get them. "Mike, be careful walking with that sheet cake, there's—"

Too late. He found the shoes, tripped over them and probably trying to keep the cake from ruining his suit, raised it up and caused it to go sliding down on top of his expertly coiffed head.

She tried to help him get cleaned up but he ordered her out of the house.

"I actually feel kind of bad about that," Jo told her husband-to-be—*husband-to-be,* what a wonderful phrase—as they walked to their cars.

"I don't know. Maybe the guy had it coming."

"What?" As she strode along she tried to match his gait, her shoes dangling from her fingers.

"You're a minister, I thought you'd be more forgiving than that."

"Forgiving, sure. But the guy was a major creep and a cheat. So he ended up with a little cake on his head."

"Don't go there." She stopped and held up her hand to try to prevent him from making the awful pun.

"Guess you could say he got his just deserts."

"You went there. I can't believe it."

"Hey." He bent down and gave her a kiss on the nose. "Nobody's perfect. Now let's go out to dinner and celebrate. I have some news to tell you before you can call your mom and sisters."

Chapter Twenty-Four

The bell over the door of the *Sun Times* hadn't stopped jangling before Peg called out, "Hey, Moxie! Heard the big news about your sister!"

"Which one?"

"The one who just got engaged."

"Again, I have to ask—*which* sister who just got engaged?"

"Are you saying that Jo . . . ?"

"The only other sister that I have—that I know of!"

"And Travis?"

"Yep."

"When?"

"Same day. Different city."

"Jo and Travis are moving to Atlanta?"

"No, she was there on business and when Mom and I asked him to go up there to tell her about Kate and Vince, well . . ."

"Ahh. Young love." Peg looked off into the far unseen and sighed.

Moxie laughed at her overplayed reaction. "I'm so glad you're back at work, Peg."

"Thanks, not just for saying that but for helping facilitate it."

Hunt had welcomed the whole staff back to their positions even though he really needed to cut jobs to give the budget a jump start. When two part-timers chose not to return in favor of finding work elsewhere, he had promised them if the paper ever had more work than they could handle, he'd ask them first if they wanted to pick up a few spare dollars. "It's all Hunt."

Peg shook her head. "The guy had potential. I'll grant you that but you know what they say —behind every great man there's a woman."

"Well, if you see the woman behind Hunt," Moxie said in her own pointed way of distancing herself from Peg's implication that Moxie was that woman, "tell her to give him a shove in any direction. I need to talk to him."

"Uh-huh." Peg's incredulity showed in the quirk of her lips, the lift of her eyebrow and the sharp, sure snorting quality of her harrumph. "You had to come through the newspaper office to talk to the man?"

"About newspaper business, I do." She dug into the backpack she'd hauled in with her and withdrew a yellow legal pad. "I've come by to run a For Rent ad on the house on Dream Away Bay Court now that Gentry and Pera have decided to head to Miami."

"He took the job then?" Santa Sofia had no

secrets, it seemed. "How's Vince taking the moving plans?"

"Better than he's taking having to cope with wedding plans." Moxie laughed. "He's campaigning for an elopement."

"No way!"

"I know! They wait more than twenty years and he thinks Kate will settle for anything less than the fancy white dress and all the guests? I don't think so."

Peg rolled her eyes in a way that conveyed the general sentiment women feel when they give a weary exhale and say, "Men!"

"About that ad." Moxie dived back into her backpack to try to find a pen.

"You don't have to see Hunt for that, you know. I can take the info and turn it in for you. We have forms up here and everything."

Moxie couldn't decide if Peg sounded coy or smug or amused. Maybe some combination of the three? It didn't matter, too much. In a town with no secrets, little things like people making conjectures about your love life could have some effect on your personal life, or lack of one. She glanced at the sign Never Assume and sighed. Apparently that only applied to hard news stories, not to the feasibly juicy personal-interest kind.

"I am well aware of the procedure for running an ad," she reminded Peg in her best businesswoman's voice. "This is what I want to see Hunt about."

She flashed the yellow legal pad filled with her handwriting.

"A manifesto for saving the *Sun Times*?"

"Sorry, no." Moxie's shoulders slumped a bit. She really hadn't come up with any substantive suggestions on that front, other than working to make Hunt a bigger part of the Santa Sofia community. "But this won't hurt. It's an exclusive."

"Wow. An exclusive! On what?"

"Only the inside story with all the details announcing a very much anticipated pair of engagements."

"Whoa, that is hot stuff." Peg gave a giggle and a wink. "The only thing I can imagine would make it more of a story would be if all three sisters had such an announcement."

"Stop it, Peg, I've only known the man a short time."

"Sure. Too soon for rings and things." She plucked a form from the basket on the counter by the opening in the wall. "But not too soon to know you want the rings *and* the things."

"Peg! That's not the kind of thing you should go around saying."

She held her hands out to emphasize her stationary position at the receptionist area. "I'm not going around anywhere."

287

"You don't have to. Everyone in town eventually comes around to you." Moxie took the form and tucked it in her bag to fill out later. "Hunt and I are just—"

"Perfect for each other."

"Peg!"

"Oh, Moxie, don't let's be childish. You're over thirty . . ."

"Just thirty," Moxie corrected.

"You've had a cake with thirty candles?"

"Um, yes."

"Like I was saying, you're over thirty. Old enough to know what you want. And what you don't want. You dated Lionel for how long?"

"Too long."

"Exactly. But y'all never made that leap because you both knew."

"He proposed plenty."

"A man only keeps proposing when he keeps getting turned down because he knows he *will* be turned down."

That sure sounded like Lionel. Moxie conceded that with a tilt of her head.

"Now you've met this man and something in you knows."

"Knows what?" Hunt came strolling up behind Peg, seemingly unaware of Moxie standing on the other side of the wall opening.

"I'm glad you're here, Mr. Editor," Peg chirped as she scooted herself to one side to give him a glimpse out the receptionist's window. "Have we got a scoop for you."

Hunt ducked down to look. When he saw Moxie, his whole face lit up. "Hey!"

You just know.

Moxie couldn't contain her own smile, or her racing pulse or the heat rising in her cheeks. She gave him a finger-wriggling wave. "Hi."

"What's the big scoop? Don't tell me . . . let me guess." He held his hands up to stop her then used them to pan the breadth of an invisible headline unfurling before him. "World Energy Crisis Resolved By Discovery of Limitless Oil Reserves Found in Kitchen of Billy J's Bait Shack Seafood Buffet."

Moxie giggled. "This is bigger than that!"

"Bigger than a world crisis?"

"The world will always be struggling, Hunt. Haven't you read your Bible? That's hardly news." She shook her head then lifted up the pad filled with the information she'd meticulously copied from her sisters. "But love triumphing over adversity and human shortcomings? Now that's news that sells papers."

"Well, come on back and tell me about it. We need to sell all the papers we can."

Chapter Twenty-Five

"Two weddings?" Hunt asked.

"Two engagements. There's a difference."

"Technically, yes, I suppose, but you expect them both to end in weddings, right?"

"No, I expect them to culminate in the beginnings of two wonderful marriages," Moxie said with a smile.

"Right."

"But this story is just to announce the engagements," she explained. "After the weddings, you can run a separate story."

He nodded. "Are these expected to be long engagements?"

His reference made her realize he didn't want to commit to a story for a newspaper with an uncertain fate.

"Things not going any better for the *Sun Times?*"

"Despite your best efforts to help me integrate into the community, which resulted in my broadening my résumé in ways I'd never anticipated, including bingo calling at the Senior Citizens' Center, judging a sand castle building contest for middle schoolers and drinking so much sweet tea I dream of surfing on the stuff—"

"People just don't understand how much you suffer for your work," she teased.

"Despite all that, no, things are not much better for the *Sun Times*. Subscriptions are up slightly and we've had some new advertisers, but we've lost some, too."

"I've been busy with Dad being sick, but now that he's on the mend, I can put in a good word with those potential accounts if you think it will help."

"Thanks, but I can do my own sales. I *want* to do my own sales."

"Good." She liked knowing he wanted to get out and circulate among the people of the town she loved. This hands-on approach to running the newspaper could go a long way toward the big plan to keep it solvent. "That's a positive public-relations move for you."

"You mean for the *Sun Times*," he corrected.

"When will you get it through your head that in a town this small, businesses and endeavors are so intertwined with the people who run them that they cannot be separated or compartmentalized?" She quirked a brow. "My dad *is* the Bait Shack. Travis is the Wayside Chapel. Lionel and his dad before him are the Urgent Care Clinic."

"So you're saying that making associations . . .

friendships, really, are what keeps small towns afloat?"

"One of the things, yes."

He shook his head. "That's not the Reinhardt Media way."

"Are you Reinhardt Media?"

His gaze connected with hers.

"The way my dad is what he does? The way Travis is? If you stopped working for your family business, operating the Reinhardt way, would the corporate machine throw a cog?"

She could practically see his mental process as he turned that thought over once, then again.

He exhaled and shook his head. "No. No, I'm not."

Moxie went to him and gave him a hug. "I didn't think so."

"I am not my family business." He folded his arms around her and rested the side of his face against her hair. "I love them, but my working with them neither defines the quality of job, the significance of our relationships or me as a person."

Moxie pulled away, just enough to look him in the eye again and smile. "I love my family but I'm my own person. Who would have thought to look at you and me that we'd both need to learn the same lesson?"

"Spoken like someone who had the faith I could learn." He kissed her lightly. "Of course, that doesn't save the *Sun Times,* you know."

She touched his cheek. "You'll get those advertisers back."

"Maybe." He shook his head. "But what do I do about the places that have closed shop recently? Some of them I can't replace. Others won't be running any ads until they see if we get enough snowbird traffic this winter to make it worth their while to open again."

"We?"

"Hmm?"

"You said 'we.' Until they see if 'we' get enough snowbird traffic."

"I meant the town, Santa Sofia."

"Of which you have already begun to feel a part . . . of." The grammar evaded her but neither she nor Hunt could escape from the truth. "After just a short time here in sweet, idyllic Santa Sofia, you consider this home, or at least a home away from home."

"Home," he murmured, seemingly trying it out.

"I hope I played a part in making you feel like . . . that . . . you . . ."

He kissed her again, saving her from a new grammatical entanglement—and involved her in quite another kind of entanglement altogether.

"Hunt! You shouldn't do that."

"I shouldn't?" He looked worried.

She laughed lightly. "Not in your office, silly. And after that big talk about people in a small town being synonymous with their workplace? What would people think?"

"That I've just met the most terrific girl in the world?"

When he's the right one, you know.

"About your business," she reminded him. "What kind of association would people make with you and the paper if they caught us in here kissing?"

"Maybe it won't matter, if we can't keep the place of business open."

"Exactly!" She stepped back and straightened her white cotton shirt and smoothed her hand down her blue-and-white striped skirt. "They will think the paper fell apart because you didn't have your mind on your work."

"Okay, okay." He smiled. "I'll get back to work. You had an article you wanted to submit?"

Moxie reached for the yellow pad that she had laid on his desk. "I don't know."

"Something wrong?"

"After all this talk about lost ads, I wonder . . ."

"What?"

"Maybe I should hold this for a few days and see if I can't pin my sisters down to a wedding date—get all the info we can into the paper and out to the town while there's still a paper to get out."

"Wedding date? Singular?" he queried.

"Yeah. They plan to get married on the same

date after the holidays. Probably the first week of January."

"I've heard of that. A double wedding, right?"

"No, two weddings, each separate and significant but one right after the other." Moxie flipped a page of the legal pad up and slipped free the pair of photos she had paper-clipped to the cardboard underneath. "See, Kate and Vince met on the beach, almost twenty years ago."

He took their picture and studied it a moment.

"So they want to get married on the beach." She handed him the photo of Travis and Jo. "Their future lies at the Traveler's Wayside Chapel."

"Which is on the beach." He took the photo but his gaze lifted and fixed on Moxie. "Pretty convenient."

"Yeah. Unless you are the single kid sister of two brides who each expect you to do maid of honor duties, including hosting showers, dealing with the throngs of media—" she gave him a grin and a wink "—and donning not one, but possibly two atrocious, froufrou hoop-skirted seafoam green or cotton-candy pink bridesmaid dresses."

"That I'd like to see."

"I'd invite you to be my date, but January?" She let out a long, soft whistle. "Sounds like a long way off in newspaper-not-going-belly-up time."

He chuckled. "I'll still be here."

"You think the *Sun Times*—"

"I can't say for sure."

"You mean you might actually consider staying on in Santa Sofia even if the *Sun Times* folds?"

"Actually, if the *Sun Times* folds, I have a plan."

"Tell me," she insisted.

"Can't."

"Please?"

"Nope."

"If you tell me, I'll make sure you're invited."

"It's on the beach in Santa Sofia. Everyone will be invited," he reminded her.

"Okay, then, if you tell me, I'll make sure you aren't recruited to dress up in whatever getup they pick for groomsmen and be a party to all the foolishness."

"Marriage foolishness? I didn't think you'd feel that way."

"I don't. I have a lot of respect for marriage. I hope one day to be married myself." *To you, if things go well.* She held her tongue on that matter while she continued to hold his gaze. "It's the whole circus surrounding weddings that I don't have much patience with."

"You didn't dream of being a bride as a kid?"

"No. As a kid I dreamt of . . ." She grew instantly somber as she said softly, "Of having a real family."

"That's the important thing," he said, brushing her hair back off her temple. "Marriage is the first step in starting your *own* family."

She lifted her face so that he could kiss her again but the sound of Peg coming through the hallway made them move apart. After the receptionist went past the half-open door, Moxie gave him a playful punch in the arm. "So whatcha doing this evening?"

"You offering to cook for me?"

"No. But I will try to see if I can make sure your meal comes out of the deep fat fryer that was most recently cleaned at the Bait Shack."

"The Bait Shack. Pretty fancy digs. What's the occasion?"

"Celebrating the engagements. Oh, and Gentry Merchant's new job in Miami."

"If I come . . ."

If? She hadn't imagined he wouldn't. "Uh-huh?"

"Do I have to pour the sweet tea?"

"Not if you tell me what your plans are."

He worked his arm around the way a baseball pitcher might before taking the mound for a big game. "Hey, a little service never hurt anybody."

The meal went great. Hunt did pour his share of sweet tea and ate his fill of fried food.

Billy J made an appearance, though Dodie made sure he did not jeopardize his health by whisking him off after the many rounds of toasts and family photos.

Jo and Travis, Kate and Vince, and Pera and Gentry all looked so happy.

Moxie wasn't exactly miserable herself.

In fact, she so enjoyed Hunt's company that she didn't even notice Lionel's arrival until Jo, who suddenly up and demanded that she and Kate go with her to the ladies' room, pointed it out.

"I think he's on a date," Jo whispered when she got them all gathered outside the restroom door.

"How can you can tell?" Kate wanted to know, leaning on her cane and straining her neck to catch a peek.

"He didn't wear his lab coat," Moxie told them, waited a moment then joined them in a good-natured laugh. Then she, too, stole a look at the couple. "Is that one of the residents who pulls shifts at the Urgent Care Clinic sometimes?"

"Jealous?" Kate wanted to know.

"No, worried," Moxie replied.

"About what?"

"That Lionel might fall for a lady doctor then want to cut her into the clinic, you know, keep it in the family, and in doing so squeeze you out."

"First, it will take a long time before she's got the financial resources to buy me out and second . . . maybe I will be ready for her to do just that," Kate said.

"What? That sounds like . . ." Jo cut herself off after a sharp look from her big sister. She shifted her tone and tactic to finish, ". . . the old Katie talking."

"Just the opposite. The old Katie never could settle, always thought something better could be found in the next job, the next relationship, the next town. But this Kate, she's here to stay and who knows, maybe when it's time for Lionel to get a new partner I'll be ready to spend some time in my own home, raising my own family."

"Oh, Kate!" Both Jo and Moxie hugged her. "That would be so wonderful."

"I'm not going anywhere," Kate reassured them. "We're a family now."

Moxie stepped back. "We are a family, aren't we?"

"We always have been." Kate held Jo's hand and stroked Moxie's cheek.

"Well, then, you know what families do?"

Both sisters looked at her, confused.

"When someone needs us, we go." She took each of them by one hand and gave a tug. "Let's move this party to my dad's house. Our family should really be together at a time like this."

Chapter Twenty-Six

On the day after Christmas a twenty-four-page plus extra photo insert edition of the *Santa Sofia Sun Times* hit newspaper stands. In it, along with biographies of all past and present staff members, award-winning and sentimental favorite photos and the top news stories spanning the paper's sixty-three-year history, was a letter from the editor.

To the Good People of Santa Sofia
R. Hunt Diamante
Sun Times editor

First and foremost I must say thank you to our subscribers and advertisers for the support you have given to this paper and to me personally. I will never forget how you have rallied around our cause. In doing so, you have restored my faith in the power of the fourth estate to touch people's lives. You have convinced me once again of the basic human dignity and decency of those people who so often the tension-hungry pop media overlooks.

Next I want to thank not just my staff, but also to acknowledge everyone who ever worked on this fine enterprise. Your tireless efforts aimed at keeping the public informed despite every kind of obstacle from natural disaster to national syndication buyouts, through wartime, peace, prosperity and economic turmoil are among the noblest of uses of the power and influence of any form of media.

On a personal note, thank you to the friends and makeshift family that I have made here in this lovely town for helping me find my sense of direction and keep my sense of humor—even if they did convince me to lose my beard, which I still miss horribly. Thank you to Vince Merchant, a good friend and sounding board. To Travis Brandt, my new pastor and sometimes surfing buddy. To the Cromwell family and Billy J Weatherby, who fed me and gave me a home away from home—in other words, a real home. And to Maxine—y'all know who I mean. Nobody really thinks I would use this paper to post a written profession of my affections or my plans regarding her, do they? Besides, if anyone really has any questions about how I feel about that girl, just watch the way I look at her. 'Nuff said.

Last, I find myself in one of the most awkward and frustrating situations a newspaper man can encounter—being at a loss for words. It has been a long and winding road to this day. I wish I had some clever or breathtakingly wise words to impart that might stand forever as a monument to my skill as a writer and my passion for the people of this fine community. I just can't think of anything more to say than thank you, Santa Sofia, you are the best.

It was the final edition of the *Santa Sofia Sun Times*.

Chapter Twenty-Seven

You are cordially invited . . .

"I think it should have said, 'you are casually invited,'" Hunt whispered to Moxie as they stood as part of a small semicircle of onlookers gathered on the beach on a warm January afternoon watching Kate and Vince take their vows.

They had decided against the maid of honor and best man type of wedding, opting instead for their families to gather around them to all share in the moment. Kate wore a diaphanous dress in a warm white shade called candlelight. The gathered skirt ended five inches from her feet so it did not drag in the sand but also did not hide the purple cast on her foot from her latest surgery. It was classic in style with a gorgeous hand-embroidered and beaded belt. She wore daisies in her hair, and the biggest smile Moxie had ever seen on her tanned face.

Vince looked great, too, in canvas-colored jeans and a pale blue shirt with a smudge of chocolate cookie on the shoulder from holding Fabbie as they had all made their way to this spot.

"Sorry about not being more clear about what to wear," Moxie whispered back to the man in the suit and tie . . . and shoes. The only person in attendance wearing any of those. "I thought you'd know that a wedding on the beach is always barefoot—especially if the bride is in a cast!"

"Guess the pages of my wedding etiquette book with that info on them were stuck together or something," Hunt shot back.

She turned to him and smiled. "You are so cute."

"I don't feel cute. I feel overdressed."

"Shh." She patted his arm. "They're taking their vows."

Travis, who had railed a bit against the traditional wording of the service the couple chose, raised the book with the vows in it and began, "Do you, Kate—"

"Yes!"

"Finally!" Vince grinned.

The group laughed.

Travis was taken aback for only a second then embraced with gusto the way this pair was going to make the traditional vows their own.

"Vince?"

"Me, too. Um, I do." He held both of Kate's hands in his and never once let his gaze stray from hers as he asked, "Can I kiss the bride now?"

"Don't you want to give your vows?" Travis asked.

"Of course, sure." Vince nodded. "It's just that we're not kids who don't know what we're getting into. We love each other, we honor each other, we're committed to one another. We're a family."

"And you said you couldn't write your own vows." Travis chuckled then turned to Kate. "You agree with everything he just said?"

"Absolutely, but I do want to add one thing." She looked up at Vince and spoke with a new firmness as she promised, "I will never leave you. You are stuck with me. No running away on my part and if you try running yourself, I will follow you."

"Fair enough." Vince started to lean down to kiss her.

Travis stuck his hand out. "Hey, we're not at that part yet."

"Can we get to that part then? You know the quicker we get done with this, the quicker it's your turn at this wedding thing and then . . ."

"Cake!" Jo intervened before her almost brother-in-law reminded everyone again that they all had honeymoon reservations.

The group laughed. Travis wrapped up the ceremony and they all moved to the chapel to do it all again, only with Travis and Jo. A few other attendees donned shoes for the event.

Jo was among the shoeless, however. It was symbolic, she said. And everyone felt moved by her choice when, after coming in from the sandy beach, the couple followed the example of Christ and washed off the feet of their guests before they entered the sanctuary.

Jo was lovely and Travis handsome. They took their vows in the quiet of twilight enveloping the chapel. By the end, they spoke their vows by candlelight so dim that they were only outlines to their guests. Outlines standing so close that they appeared as one form and it was clear they saw only one another, the glow of the candles and the gleam of the cross on the altar before them.

Dodie cried at both weddings and Billy J whooped both times he heard the pronouncement, "You are now husband and wife." Adding the second time, "Two down, one to go!"

Moxie was mortified.

Hunt just laughed.

She tried not to read too much into that. After all, the paper had folded just ten days earlier and he still hadn't divulged his plans.

"So what's next for you?" became a familiar refrain at Billy J's Bait Shack Seafood Buffet, where they naturally held the receptions.

Hunt always deflected the question amicably, making a joke or spinning an outrageous tale of what lay ahead for him that caught the listener up only until they realized he was giving them the